CHRISTMAS IN THE BAY

Maddie Jones runs a bookshop in the beautiful St Nicholas Bay. Devoted to her business, she's forgotten what it's like to have a romantic life — until Ben Cartwright arrives, and reminds her of what she's missing. But Ben isn't being entirely honest about what brings him to town — and when his professional ambition threatens Maddie's livelihood, their relationship seems doomed. When a flash flood descends on the Bay, all the community must pull together — will Ben stay or go?

Books by Jo Bartlett
in the Linford Romance Library:

NO TIME FOR SECOND BEST

JO BARTLETT

CHRISTMAS IN THE BAY

Complete and Unabridged

LINFORD
Leicester

First published in Great Britain in 2015

First Linford Edition
published 2016

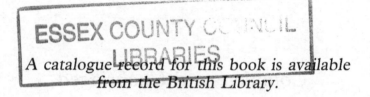

A catalogue record for this book is available
from the British Library.

ISBN 978–1–4448–3088–0

Published by
F. A. Thorpe (Publishing)
Anstey, Leicestershire

Set by Words & Graphics Ltd.
Anstey, Leicestershire
Printed and bound in Great Britain by
T. J. International Ltd., Padstow, Cornwall

This book is printed on acid-free paper

1

Maddie closed the door to the shop and took from her bag a bunch of keys that a jailor in a maximum-security prison would have been proud of. Turning all three of the locks, she shivered. It was getting colder, and goose pimples had spread across her skin, even beneath her winter coat. Her breath hung in clouds in the air and specks of ice dotted across the pavement, sparkling in the reflection of the streetlight above her head. There was no denying it — midwinter was fast approaching, bringing Christmas with it.

'What have you got hidden away in that shop of yours that needs to be locked up so tight?' The voice behind her was familiar; amusement evident in the tone.

'Only all my hopes and dreams.' Maddie smiled as she turned to face

Kate Harris, a teacher from the local primary school, who also happened to be one of her best customers. Kate was always popping in to check out books — which, more often than not, she then recommended to the children in her class. Sales always shot up after one of her visits.

'Having sampled your chocolate cake, I don't blame you for locking up tight. I'm half-tempted to break in myself now to get some!' Kate smiled. 'Although you do realise that around here, someone getting more than one parking ticket in the space of a year constitutes a crime wave, don't you?'

'I know it's daft, but I guess it's just a hangover from my old life — even after more than three years of living in St Nicholas Bay. My flat in London was broken into three times altogether, and sometimes I still forget I inhabit such a different world these days.'

'Really?' Kate laughed. 'Even with Christmas songs playing in every shop

2

in the high street from Halloween onwards?'

'Yes, unbelievably, even with that!' Maddie had almost stopped noticing the Christmas music altogether by the beginning of December. When you lived in a town that focused on the season of goodwill all year round, it was easy for the things that usually made it so distinct to start fading into the background. 'And, let's face it, you could hardly live here unless you loved all of that.'

Visiting her grandparents in St Nicholas Bay, when she'd been much younger, had always been exciting. At home, she was banned from mentioning Christmas until the beginning of December — at the earliest. She'd be met with a thin-lipped grimace from her mother if she began circling in the toy catalogue the things she most dreamed of owning before the allotted slot for writing up her Christmas list.

Her grandparents — as most grandparents tend to be — were much more indulgent about everything, including Christmas. Perhaps it was because they lived in St Nicholas Bay, where legend had it that Charles Dickens had written some of the scenes for *A Christmas Carol*; or perhaps it was because they enjoyed reliving their own childlike excitement through her. Whatever the reason behind it, those times staying with her grandparents had been amongst the happiest of her entire childhood. So maybe it was no surprise she'd settled in St Nicholas Bay as an adult. The town where she'd grown up had only been ten minutes away from the Bay, but it might as well have been a different world. And the years she'd spent living in London were like time in an another universe altogether.

'You're right; luckily, I've always loved Christmas. Just as well in my job, as the children seem to start planning for it when they come back after the summer holidays in September. Speaking of which, my whole class has been talking about your window display.' Kate gestured towards the scene Maddie had set up in the window — a fireside hung with stockings bulging with gifts, a Christmas tree barely visible beneath the fairy lights draped in circles around it, and what looked like Santa's snow-covered boots just emerging from the bottom of the chimney. 'It's fantastic!'

'Thanks. I have to admit I'm like a big kid myself with all this.' Maddie laughed again. 'In fact that's where I'm headed now, to the big craft shop at the retail park in Canterbury. I should be up in the flat doing some of the book-keeping, but this is much more fun!'

'I would say don't spend too much, but since I can't wait to see what you come up with next, I don't want to put you off your stroke!' Kate gave a little wave as she turned to leave, calling over her shoulder when she was twenty feet or so away: 'And the best thing is, it will give me an excuse to pop in over the next day or two, and have another slice of that chocolate cake!'

★ ★ ★

By the next morning, Maddie had created a mural across one wall of the shop, complete with a train which she'd cut from different-coloured cards, laden with presents and with cotton-wool balls of smoke floating up from the funnel. She'd been up until the early hours decorating the shop, and baking another batch of gingerbread men for the mother-and-toddler group who met there every Tuesday. Merging her two passions — cooking and reading — had been a happy accident, of course. The name of the shop, on the other hand, had never been in question. It was only ever going to be 'Cecil's Adventures'.

Almost all of the shops in St Nicholas Bay drew heavily on the town's association with *A Christmas Carol* — everything from Tiny Tim's Toys to Marley's Chains, the local hardware store, had gone with the theme. When Maddie had inherited the money to buy the fifty-year lease to her shop, she'd received all sorts of suggestions about what to call it — from Scrooge's Stories to Cratchit Books, and everything in between. Only she hadn't wanted to go down that route: there was one person to thank for her new venture, and one person to credit for her love of books; and that was Cecil Jones, her late grandfather.

Cecil had always worked in the tiny library in St Nicholas Bay, until he was forced to retire when the local council decided that anyone wanting to borrow a book would have to head over to the next town, which had a much larger stock of titles. Her grandfather had never been quite the same after that, as if a light had gone out inside him. He'd ignited a similar love of books in Maddie long before his enforced retirement, though. In the school holidays, when her parents had been at work and she'd become fed up baking cakes with her grandmother, Cecil would take her to work with him. When it was quiet, as it often was, they would pick a book from the shelves together, and he'd read to her. One day they might be pirates, searching for treasure and travelling across treacherous seas; the next day they could be banqueting with Henry the Eighth, narrowly avoiding losing their heads. But every day was an adventure, and her grandfather had made the tales come alive. It wasn't until much later that she realised Cecil, who seemed to have been everywhere and know everything, had in fact hardly ever left the small town where he'd been born, and had instead spent fifty years travelling the world inside the four walls of its library.

Despite that, he'd encouraged Maddie to have adventures of her own. She'd gone travelling for almost two years, seeing lots of the places they'd read about together, before studying English Literature at university — that love of books so firmly ingrained. She'd visited her grandparents whenever she could, and took a job writing website content — to pay the rent on her shared flat — but St Nicholas Bay and those adventures with her grandfather had never been far from her thoughts.

When her grandfather died, just a year after her grandmother, her parents had realised their long-held ambition to move to the Cornish coast. At first, Maddie had been too scared to invest her inheritance in something where she risked losing it all. So she'd kept her own dreams locked up in a metaphorical box. Instead, she'd taken a job as a teaching assistant in a secondary school twenty minutes' drive from the Bay — but she couldn't stop thinking about what she really wanted. In the end, at just twenty-six, she'd finally plucked up the courage to follow her star and buy a bookshop, which she knew only too well was a huge risk in a shrinking market. Being in St Nicholas Bay meant that it had bucked the trend, though. The teashop had started off as her just offering people a drink while they browsed or read at the tables she'd provided in one corner of the shop. Now it drew people in, made her unique. When it was quiet, she'd still take out a book and be transported to a world of the writer's creation, without ever once leaving the building. So Cecil's Adventures it was, even though it didn't cash in on the Bay's famous connection, and no-one would know it was a bookshop just from seeing the name. It didn't matter: it could never have been anything else.

* * *

Ben barely resisted the urge to shout at the driver ahead of him as they slowed yet again on the narrow country roads, before coming to a stop as the bottleneck of traffic in front of them took the bends with equal caution. Drumming one hand on the steering wheel, he massaged the back of his neck with the other one. He didn't want this last assignment of the year to be a difficult one: spending any more time than he had to in this tourist trap in the middle of nowhere wasn't his idea of fun. If, as he suspected, they had Christmas music piping out of every shop he passed, he wasn't quite sure he would be responsible for his actions.

The traffic still wasn't moving, so he glanced at the file on the passenger seat beside him. Two shops would be ideal, but one would work at a push. The bigger shop, Belle's Brides, was the key; although securing Cecil's Adventures was the real challenge, and it was that which would give him his biggest bonus yet. The research had suggested that Rosie Summers, who owned the leasehold of Belle's Brides, might be willing to sell. Profits hadn't risen in line with costs, according to the company's accounts, and he knew only too well how close to the wind some of these small businesses sailed. Madeleine Jones, however, who owned the leasehold of Cecil's Adventures, wasn't going to be a pushover. Bookshops, even the huge chains, were shutting

11

down everywhere; but she was doing incredibly well, according to the figures. Still, there'd be a big budget for any offer made on the lease, and money almost always talked in the end.

'Thank God for that.' The traffic started to move at last and, as Ben followed the cars in front of him over a small stone bridge, he got his first look at St Nicholas Bay. He could admit it was pretty — his mother would probably have said 'quaint' — but the cottages reminded him far too much of what had been taken away from them twenty years before. If he ever felt guilty about pushing through a recommendation to purchase, he remembered that he was doing these people a favour. If anyone in St Nicholas Bay decided to sell their leases for the very generous offer they'd be made, they'd be almost guaranteed to make more money than they could in ten years of working six days a week, slogging their guts out — if they didn't go bankrupt first.

His phone rang, and the hands-free

facility in the car picked up the call.

'Darling, where are you?'

'Just about to try and find the hotel they've booked me into in this strange little place. It looks like a set from a movie.' Ben laughed. 'In fact, I was just thinking how much you'd love it.'

'Which means you'll hate it, then!' His mother's voice was warm, even though there was almost certainly a reprimand in there somewhere. She didn't entirely approve of what he did and she'd made it obvious she thought he should stop once they were out of trouble. Except that the success — and, if he was entirely honest, the money — had become like a drug to him. If people accused him of having a soulless job, that was their problem, not his.

'I don't *hate* the town, it's just a bit twee for me.'

'So, no twenty-four-hour takeaways, multiplex cinemas or chain stores, then?' She sighed. 'Oh, Ben, I do worry about you sometimes.'

'I know you do, but then it's your job, isn't it?'

'It is, but you're the one who's had to worry more about me over the years than you should have done, and that's the real problem.' There was that familiar note of regret in his mother's voice and it was a conversation they'd had at least a hundred times before. Nothing could change the past, so the best thing they could do was forget it; only she didn't seem able to.

'I've turned out alright, Mum. I like my job, I'm good at it, and we're all doing okay now, aren't we? We got over it, so you can stop worrying now, I promise.' He wasn't going to talk about it again. It was time for a change of subject. 'Anyway, shouldn't you be packing?'

'All done. That was why I was ringing. I wanted to thank you again for everything you did at the wedding. Richard couldn't be more delighted to have you as a stepson, and you made me so proud.' Her voice caught with emotion.

'He's a good man, Mum, and I think you're going to be really happy if you let yourself.' The satnav interrupted for a moment, giving him the information that his hotel was just up ahead on the right. 'I've got to go, but I want you to promise me that you'll enjoy your honeymoon. Oh, and — yes, before you ask, I promise I'll try to phone Will on Christmas Day, but you know what us boys are like about that sort of thing.'

'I do, and that's what worries me!' The note of panic was back in her voice again. 'You will be alright on Christmas Day without me, won't you, the pair of you?'

'Mum, I'm thirty-one and Will is twenty-five; we're not your little boys anymore.' He couldn't help laughing. 'Now, get on that boat and cruise round those Caribbean islands like it's your honeymoon!'

'And what will *you* be doing?' She

clearly wasn't going to give up that easily.

'I've had offers, Mum, and I promise I won't be sitting alone pining after your Christmas dinner — I'm sure I can find someone else who makes Brussels sprouts like bullets.' Laughing, he pulled into the car park behind the old coaching inn.

'You cheeky blighter!' She was laughing too, though; the mood lightened. 'I love you, Ben. Happy Christmas.'

'You too, Mum.' Ending the call, he checked his file again. He'd take his bags up to his room in The Quill and Ink, and then head straight down to check out the two shops. Belle's Brides was definitely first on the agenda. He had a feeling that Cecil's Adventures would be a much longer game.

2

'Come in, come in, it's freezing out there!' Becky opened the door at the top of the stairwell that led up the side of Ebenezer's Christmas Emporium to the flat above it. Like Maddie, she lived above her shop; and, because Becky's store was spread over two floors, the flat was in the roof-space of the building, so looked all the more as if it had come straight out of a Dickens novel. Becky was one of those people who loved anything old. The ornaments in the shop were true to the Victorian era of *A Christmas Carol*, and she received lots of orders from across the world as a result. She worked in the shop all the hours God sent, and it had seemed like madness to Maddie that she ran herself so ragged when she could probably make a living from the online sales alone. But Becky had admitted that it was only working in the shop and having her young son David to go home to that had kept her going after Henry's death: she was scared to give herself the chance to stop and really think about it all. Leaving the shop would also mean moving away from St Nicholas Bay, and Maddie knew that was the last thing her friend wanted.

Henry's accident had happened in the first year Cecil's Adventures had been open. Maddie had got to know the couple well in a short time, as Henry had been head of the local traders' association, and they'd both done everything they could to help her get established. So, when his car veered off the road on the Welham Valley, making his young wife a widow, Maddie had made sure she was there for Becky in whatever way she could be. Although her friend so rarely asked for help that it was down to Maddie to try and work out what she could do to offer some support. The family had been through so much, even before the accident, yet she'd never once heard Becky ask 'Why me?'. She wasn't sure if she could have been so gracious in the same situation, which only made her admire Becky more.

'I've got Chinese food, and I've asked for extra chillies on your shredded beef, so that ought to warm us up.' Maddie handed Becky the bag she'd collected from The Golden Gift restaurant on the way over. 'I got David some fortune cookies too. I didn't know if he'd still be up, but I know he loves them.'

'He tried desperately to stay awake to see you, but his eyes kept drooping closed, and in the end I had to carry him to bed. But I know one little boy who'll be asking for fortune cookies for breakfast in the morning!' Becky led the way through to the kitchen area as she spoke, where plates were already warming in the oven. The living area of the flat was open-plan, almost loft-style, and there were just three other rooms that led off it — two bedrooms and a bathroom. It wasn't the grandest of homes, but it was beautifully decorated, with stripped oak floorboards and high-sided leather chairs that looked as though they could give you a hug. It was a place Maddie always felt welcome in, even when Becky had been going through the darkest of days.

'Is he getting excited about Christmas yet?' She leant against the worktop as Becky deftly opened the food containers and the smell of shredded beef and chicken noodles wafted up, making her stomach grumble in anticipation.

'Only every minute of every day! You'd think with us running a Christmas shop he'd be pretty much immune to the whole thing, but he's more into it this year than ever before.' Becky laughed. 'I think starting in Kate's class at school last term has made him all the more enthusiastic, and he's got a part in the nativity as the innkeeper, too. He's only got one or two lines, but he's taking it all pretty seriously!'

'I can't wait to go and see him per-form.' Maddie smiled at the thought. She could just imagine the serious expression David would have on his face while he practised his lines. 'How's he doing with his Christmas list? Any ideas of what I can get him?'

'Well, having written a list of about twenty things he wants from Tiny Tim's Toys and a couple of other shops in the Bay, yours included, I took him in to Canterbury last week — and now the list is twice as long! Although he did say he'd cross everything else off if he could just have a wooden castle like the one in the window of Tiny Tim's. I spoke to Meg and that one's already sold, but she's ordered another one for me. Mind you, even though David said that about only wanting the castle, it didn't stop him wanting to go into every place in Canterbury that sold toys, books or chocolate!' She handed Maddie two glasses and a bottle of sparking water. 'In fact, he dragged me into so many shops, my feet were killing me, and we had to have a pit stop in Hemmingway's . . . ' Even as she said the words, Becky clapped a hand over her mouth.

'Tell me you didn't say that? Hemmingway's? Anywhere but there!' Maddie's eyebrows shot up beneath her fringe, almost against her will. She didn't want to react that way at the very mention of the chain of soulless coffee shops that seemed to be shutting little independent places down everywhere, but she couldn't seem to help it. 'You know that's the equivalent of me buying my Christmas decorations from a pound shop that only stocks mass-produced plastic baubles, don't you? If they have their way, they'll stamp out businesses like mine altogether, and every high street in the world will look the same.'

'I'm sorry, I know, I know, and I promise not to do it again!' Becky mimed the action of slapping the back of her own hand, and Maddie couldn't help laughing. She was pretty easy-going as a rule, but the mention of those coffee shops was one thing guaranteed to provoke a reaction.

'In that case, I promise to come off my high horse.'

'Probably not the best place to eat a takeaway, anyway!' Becky winked. 'Come on, let's eat this whilst it's hot, and you can fill me in on the gossip in the Bay.'

'With pleasure.' Maddie gave her a wry smile. 'And that's exactly the kind of personal service you'll never find in a Hemmingway's!'

★ ★ ★

Rosie Summers was Jamaican, larger than life, and had the most ready laugh of anyone Maddie had ever met. It was just over three weeks until Christmas, and she must have had alterations to do on dresses for at least a dozen December brides, as well as a rush on the party wear she sold in the shop for all the forthcoming festive events. Yet she was in Cecil's Adventures again, pondering between her two favourites — a walnut whip cupcake or a slice of lemon drizzle cake. In the end, she opted for both.

'Who's looking after the shop?' Maddie made her friend a latte, smiling to herself as she watched her assistant, Enid, lift a copy of *The Night Before Christmas* down from the shelves and take it to the reading area where a group of children waited with their parents. Enid was in her late sixties, and almost certainly helped out at the shop more because of the children's activities there than for her modest hourly rate. She was still waiting for grandchildren that hadn't arrived, and for whom she'd told Maddie she was all the more desperate since her younger sister had become a grandmother the year before.

'I've got Kayleigh in today; she's finished her dressmaking course at college for Christmas, and so she'll be in every day from now on.' Rosie grinned, and lit up the whole room. 'So

I thought I'd come in and tell you about my latest adventure!' She'd been internet dating for the past eleven months since deciding that this would be the year she'd find the man she wanted to settle down with before it was too late. She was on a mission not to be left with a bridal shop and the irony of never having had a wedding of her own. They'd taken to calling her internet dates 'adventures' in front of Kayleigh, Enid and Rosie's nineteen-year-old assistant, in case it all turned out to be a disaster. As it turned out, it had proved to be anything but; and, since there had been so many adventures, Rosie had declared that Cecil's Adventures was the only place suitable for hearing the latest instalment. Each date was recounted in great detail, an event which absolutely had to be accompanied by a large latte and at least one type of cake.

'Come on, then, fill me in. Vicarious excitement is the only kind I get these days, and Becky will be relying on your

news for her next fix of gossip too!'
Maddie ran a hand through her dark
hair and gave a half-sigh. It was true she
loved the shop, but it was all-
consuming and made it difficult to
meet anyone new, especially if they
didn't happen to venture into St
Nicholas Bay. Most of the time, she
wasn't in the slightest bit bothered.
Like her grandfather before her, she
had found a way of getting all she
needed — romance or otherwise
— between the covers of the books she
loved. Her best friend's tales were just
an added bonus.

'He's name's Simon, he's a geography teacher, and we've been seeing
each other since early November.' Rosie
looked almost shy as she spoke, and
Maddie could tell it was serious. For
her to have been dating for over a
month and not to have spilled every
bean that there was to spill, was a first.

'His second name isn't Matthews, is
it?' Maddie widened her green eyes.
She remembered him well from her

year working at the local secondary school, two towns away. If it *was* the same Simon, Rosie was definitely venturing against type, which could only be a good thing.

'Oh, my goodness, yes — that's him! I'd forgotten you worked at the school before you had the shop.' Rosie, who normally took everything in her stride, looked more worried than Maddie had ever seen her. Usually she was resolutely cheerful, whatever was going on. '*Please* don't tell me anything horrible about him, like he's married or something.'

'Simon is lovely!' Maddie reached out and closed her hand over her friend's. 'He was probably the most helpful out of everyone in my first term at the school, even though he was in another department.' She couldn't have picked anyone more perfect for Rosie if she'd chosen him herself. 'He's just an all-round good guy. The kids loved him, and he was always putting in extra hours to help anyone struggling with the subject to catch up. In fact, I'm pretty sure we'd have stayed in touch as friends when I left the school if this place hadn't completely taken over my life.'

'Oh, thank goodness! I really like him, Maddie. I mean, *really* like him! I know he's much geekier than my usual type, but I love the fact his hair looks as though he doesn't spend hours in front of the mirror, and he cares more about the kids he works with then he does about what he's wearing.' Rosie's trademark grin was firmly back in situ. 'And let me tell you this, behind those little round glasses of his, he has the most amazing blue eyes I have ever seen!'

'This is seriously exciting — a whole month of dating! So, what's next?' Maddie smiled. Rosie's excitement was infectious; and maybe, if internet dating could work out this well, she'd even give a go herself one of these days.

'Well, for one thing, I don't need so many of these books anymore, and you can put this lot in the 'recommended reads' section, for a start.' Rosie lifted a stack of well-thumbed paperbacks out of her bag and put them all on the table. They were all romance novels, the type where a happy ending was guaranteed. She'd been seriously addicted to them and had bought more than any of Maddie's other customers over the three years since Cecil's Adventures had opened. The recommended reads section was actually a second-hand-book zone, where customers could sell on their old titles, getting points towards their next book purchase for each volume they dropped off. Maddie then sold them on, and half the profits went to Dreams for David — the charitable trust the trading association had set up when Becky had been widowed and left to raise her disabled son alone.

'A stack like that will get you quite a few points towards your next book!' Maddie turned the books over, one by one. They were in good condition, so she'd be able to sell them on okay. 'Anything in mind to use them for? There's a new Mills and Boon in stock if you fancy that?'

'Not this time. There's something else I need. I might know all about the dresses and the party favours, but the rest of it's a mystery to me . . . So, what I really want is something on wedding planning!' Rosie shrieked with excitement and even Enid stopped reading to the children for a moment to look over. 'Sorry, I'm just so happy.'

'A wedding, really, after a month?' A frisson of panic gripped Maddie. Maybe feeding Rosie's passion for romance all this time had been doing a friend a disservice. Did that sort of thing actually happen in real life and turn out to be a happily-ever-after? She'd never been one to believe in love at first sight, herself. And even a month seemed a pretty short window to have any idea what someone was *really* like.

'I know it sounds crazy, and if anyone

else told me they were thinking the same after such a short time, I'd be worried too.' Rosie was still grinning. 'We're not going to rush up the aisle this week, but we've talked about it. And when you know, you know. It's not just me getting carried away by all of these, either.' She gestured towards the stack of novels she'd just set down. 'Although maybe you're the one who should think about stepping away from the novels every now and then, and trying out some real life for a change. I want you to be happy too, Mads; you deserve it.'

She'd been just about to respond, to say she'd been thinking about dipping her toe back into the dating waters after so long concentrating on the business, when the bell above the shop door pinged, interrupting them.

'Sorry to ask, since I'm not here as a customer . . . ' The man who'd just walked into the shop had the most amazing smile. ' . . . but I'm actually looking for the lady who owns the shop next door — Rosie Summers?'

'You've found her.' Rosie returned his smile, and Maddie had to press her lips together to stop herself giggling. Despite the morning's announcement about the seriousness of her relationship with Simon, Rosie was still fluttering her eyelashes in her trademark style. 'Can I ask who's looking for me?'

'My name's Ben Cartwright, and someone told me you stock some great party dresses for children? I'm after something for my niece for Christmas.' He had warm brown eyes, and he wouldn't have been safe from Rosie if he'd arrived a month earlier. Maddie tried to busy herself clearing away the rest of the romance novels from the counter, but kept sneaking a glance at him, those brown eyes drawing her in too. That was it — daydreaming over a customer was definitely a sign. She had to get a dating life of her own, or she'd be buying up all Rosie's second-hand romance novels herself before too long.

'I've got plenty of things she might like.' Rosie's eyelash-fluttering was still going strong. 'In fact, there's stuff for all the women in your family. Maybe a wife who needs a cocktail dress for a New Year's Eve party? Trust me, she'd love to open that on Christmas morning instead of yet another bottle of perfume or basket of toiletries.' Rosie raised a quizzical eyebrow, and Maddie had to admit she was good. It had taken her less than a minute to ask if he was married or not.

'No, no wife or children of my own; just a three-year-old niece, and even she came as a bit of a surprise to me — if not to my brother!' Ben laughed.

'In that case, after you've chosen something from my shop, you should have a look in here. Maddie has some great books for kids, and you could be the best uncle in the world if you shopped in both our stores for her Christmas presents!' Rosie stood up, only crumbs left from the two cakes that had been side by side on her plate minutes earlier. Maddie suppressed another smile; if Rosie always put this much effort into being a saleswoman, she'd be raking the money in, but it hadn't been her main motivation for a long time. In fact, Maddie had often worried her friend would sell up. She'd miss her more than she cared to admit if she did. Maybe now she had Simon, she'd concentrate on the shop a bit more. Although, if Maddie had to guess, she'd bet that Rosie would spend most of her time trying on the new wedding gowns that arrived in the shop instead.

'That sounds like a good plan. I could certainly afford to earn some brownie points as an uncle.' Ben turned towards Maddie and smiled. 'I'll see you later, then?'

'You will.' Lowering her eyes, she busied herself wiping down the surface in front of her, where the books had been resting, slightly concerned about how much she was hoping Ben *would* come back. Perhaps buying into all this instant romance stuff was catching? Best to sell on Rosie's stack of novels as quickly as possible — just in case.

★ ★ ★

Ben followed Rosie Summers into her shop, sure that he'd chosen the right tactic. His instant assessment when he'd stepped inside Cecil's Adventures was that simply announcing he worked for Hemmingway's would have been a recipe for disaster. Maddie Jones looked like a woman with a passion for what she did; that much was evident in the place as soon as he stepped inside. He would have loved Cecil's Adventures when he was younger, before he discovered that real life was nothing like what you read about in books — where the kids in the stories never ended up in a hostel with their mum and younger brother, having lost everything including their dad. No, in books, there was always a knight on a noble steed or a fairy godmother to sort it all out.

No-one ever had to claw their way out of poverty all by themselves.

Maddie was striking, too; that raven-black hair, with her pale skin and green eyes, might have made her a bewitching character in one of those very fairy tales. It was inevitable there'd be some guy in the picture, wanting to put his oar into the decision she should make about whether to sell the lease for Cecil's Adventures or not. His research had suggested both women were unmarried, but that didn't mean that Maddie wasn't in a relationship. No, it was definitely best to play this softly, softly; and he had a feeling that Rosie was the sort who might be only too willing to share a bit more detail about her friend's life. In fact, he was counting on it.

3

Just as Ben had expected, Rosie Summers had chatted easily about all manner of things whilst they'd worked out exactly which dress it was that his niece would most like for Christmas — something Ben would have been completely clueless about on his own. Within the space of half an hour he'd discovered that Rosie had a new boyfriend, who she hoped was about to become a new fiancé, and that she was heartily sick of working six days a week and missing out on weekends with him. Ben silently thanked whatever trick of serendipity had made that happen, just at the right time . . . for him.

He'd also found out, much to his surprise, that Maddie was single. And, much more as he might have expected, that she was a workaholic who was passionate about making Cecil's Adventures a success. He'd also discovered she'd inherited the money to start the business from her beloved grandfather — which meant that convincing her to sell would be the sort of challenge he got paid so well for.

If he'd been in a different job, he might have offered Rosie some advice on how to make the most of Belle's Brides. It was obvious her passion wasn't in the business; and, whilst she had a good selection of items, the shop didn't make the most of the space or the beautiful bay window that looked out on to the street outside. There was a large wooden chest in the middle of the window display, painted white, with several of the party dresses just draped over it. The trunk could have been opened up, with the dresses placed on wires between it and the ceiling, almost as if they were bursting out of a hidden treasure chest. The trunk could do the job, although he'd seen much better workmanship. He'd even made better once upon a time, but that had been a different life. Either way, the dress nestling at the bottom of the bag he was now holding had been a worthwhile purchase for the information it had gleaned.

★ ★ ★

As Ben opened the door of Cecil's Adventures, the smell of gingerbread filled his senses. There was a group of children animatedly putting together a gingerbread house, supervised by Maddie. Her dark hair fell into her eyes as she leant down, and she pushed it back, laughing at something one of the children had said. This place was clearly much more than a bookshop, and to Maddie, it was obviously much more than a job. This might be his biggest challenge yet.

He moved towards the counter, where a woman with tight grey curls and cheeks like shiny red apples served him the requested cappuccino, and offered him a gingerbread man to accompany it. If he'd still been a believer, he might have convinced himself she was Mother Christmas — moonlighting — and he could see why the children loved it so much in the shop.

Watching Maddie from a distance, Ben tried not to catch her eye. It was much better just to observe, try to work out what made her tick and what might give him an in to start the negotiations. By the time the gingerbread house was finished, he could see what a great sales technique the activity had been. Beside the counter, while he was ordering his coffee, he'd noticed two piles of books. One was one of those 'how to' books on making your own gingerbread house, and the other was a child's activity pack, which contained a gingerbread biscuit-cutter, a recipe book, a small rolling pin, some ingredients and a child's apron. Almost all of the parents who'd arrived to pick up their children bought copies of both books. Every child went away with a smile on their face, a gingerbread man — wrapped in cellophane with green and red ribbon tied at the top — and an almost certain desire to return to Cecil's Adventures as soon as they could. Whatever else Maddie might be, she was pretty darn good at this Christmas stuff.

'Sorry, I didn't realise you were waiting all this time.' She came straight across to his table as soon as the last of the children were gone. There was a streak of icing sugar on her cheek, where one of the children had enthusiastically tucked straight into his gingerbread man and then given her a big thank-you hug. Ben had to fight the urge to reach across and wipe it off.

'No problem, and I guess I could quite easily have picked out some books myself, only Rosie waxed so lyrical about you being an expert that I thought I'd wait. This whole *being the uncle of the year* thing is quite an appealing idea. Although I know it's a lot to ask, expecting such a personal service when I'll probably only be buying a handful of books. I'm sure you don't do that for everyone.' He raised his cup. 'In any case, the waiting was a pleasure. The coffee's great, and I could see how much the kids were enjoying the Christmas activities. It reminded me of when I still thought it was fun.' He had no idea why that last comment had slipped out; he certainly hadn't meant it to.

'I always try to give a personal service where I can: it means people come back again and again, and don't just buy everything online. You need something different to survive, these days. It's all about those little personal touches and knowing what the customer wants, even before they do. For example, for you, I'm pretty sure I must have a book here that can help remind you that Christmas can be fun, even when it isn't about the man in the big red coat anymore.' Whether she'd deliberately glossed over his comment or actually misunderstood him, he didn't know, but he was glad she didn't ask him to elaborate. What would he have said anyway? That Christmas was ruined the year his father had died and left them without a penny to their names, exposing a life that had been built on a house of cards? 'The good news is that you get to relive it all over again with your little niece now, which is wonderful, and I'm sure we can find some books that will really help with that.' She smiled again, and he had a strange feeling he'd end up buying anything she suggested. He liked her already, which was something he hadn't quite bargained for.

Following her around the shop she clearly knew like the back of her hand, they chatted about his niece and the things she was interested in. Ben couldn't bring himself to admit that he wasn't quite sure, since he'd spent far too much time working and far too little with his only brother and his family. So he kept it vague, and Maddie helped where she could.

'Most three-year-old girls seem to like the Lettice books, and everyone loves the Gruffalo, of course.' Maddie grinned. 'Oh, and sometimes *In the Night Garden*, but I think we can blame TV for that. It's our job to make sure they're exposed to other influences.'

'What do you suggest? A bit of Dickens, since he's local, or maybe even Shakespeare?' Ben returned the smile and watched as her full lips curved in response.

'I'm not sure we want to go that far, but we could start with *The BFG* by Roald Dahl. Is that how *you* were raised, then? On a diet of Shakespeare from the age of three?'

'More or less!' He couldn't help laughing, since she'd inadvertently been so spot on. 'In fact, my mum chose both mine and my brother's names because of her obsession with Shakespeare. He got off quite lightly, being William, and we've always called him Will. I wasn't quite so lucky, since I got the name of the hero in her favourite play, *Much Ado About Nothing*. So I'm really Benedick, rather than Ben — but please don't spread that around!'

'That's a great name! Anyway, it could be a heck of a lot worse — just think, you could have been something like Tybalt or Mercutio!'

''I suppose, when you put it like that, I did get off lightly.'

'So, what's the deal with Shakespeare, then? Is your mum just a fan?' Maddie looked at him steadily, as though she really wanted to know.

'Mum used to teach English and Drama before she had us, before . . . ' He realised he'd been about to tell her something of his own childhood, something that almost no-one outside his family knew about, and he had no idea why. Maybe she was just one of those people you wanted to confide in, but he'd never been the sort for deep and meaningful conversations — especially with total strangers. Whatever it was, he'd have to watch not to let his guard down. There was something about her, something that made him want to tell her things no-one needed to know. 'Before she gave all that up.'

'I think it's great; so much better than being called John or something like that. It makes you a bit more unique.'

'Well, my brother seems to be carrying on the tradition, since my niece's name is Beatrice, after the heroine in *Much Ado About Nothing*. Will did a Master's in English Literature too, so it's just me who's the black sheep of the family.'

'What is it that you do, then, that's so different from the rest of your family?' She handed him another book as she spoke, their hands brushing for a second, and he had to gather his thoughts before he could answer.

'Buying premises for a catering company, combining small shops into larger single units, that sort of thing.' He shrugged. 'Boring but true.'

'Is that what you're doing here,

looking for some commercial premises?' She eyed him suspiciously. 'There's not much that comes up for lease around here.'

'I'm looking for residential this time.' The lie tripped off Ben's tongue, but it was too early to be honest. It was always a game, knowing exactly when to show his hand. He had to have a reason for staying in town, though. No-one would believe he'd booked a hotel for two weeks just to do his Christmas shopping. 'In fact, it's personal. I'm looking for somewhere to live.' He thought briefly of the cottage he'd seen on his way into town, and shook himself; going down that particular lane of memories wouldn't do him any good.

'In that case, I might be able to help you. Is it a rental property you're looking for?' The warm smile was back on Maddie's face as he nodded in response. 'One of the mums who came in this morning told me she's been offered a new job in Dubai, and the whole family are going out there for two years. I think she's planning to lease the place while they're gone, but she might even be willing to sell up if the price is right. Although, if she does, it won't be cheap. Residential property is almost as tricky to come by around here as the commercial stuff.'

'Wow, the service you offer here really is amazing — bookshop, tearoom, and now an estate agency? Looks like today's my lucky day!'

'It could be. Especially if we can secure you that Uncle of the Year award, too.' She reached forward and handed him a copy of *The Gruffalo*, just as she'd promised. 'This one is David's absolute favourite book, and so it comes highly recommended.'

'Who's David?' He took the book from her, trying to read the expression on her face. Perhaps Rosie hadn't been as informative as she might have been, if Maddie had a child that her friend hadn't mentioned. Having a child in a local school would make it much more difficult to persuade her sell the lease — it could be a game-changer.

'That's David.' Maddie gestured towards a poster pinned to the side of one of the bookstands. 'He's five, and loves everyone and everything, but especially *The Gruffalo*. Particularly when I read it to him, complete with a range of silly voices.'

'Is he your son?' Ben looked at the photo, on a poster advertising a fundraiser for something called David's Dreams. He was a cheeky-looking little boy, with a mop of unruly red hair and bright blue eyes, and a hearing aid clearly visible in the photograph.

'No, he's Becky's son. She owns Ebenezer's Christmas Emporium, two doors up. They sell traditional Christmas decorations.' Maddie's face lit up when she spoke about the little boy. 'I wish he was mine sometimes, though! The two of them have been through a really tough time in the last few years. David contracted meningitis: it was touch and go for a while, and he suffered some quite serious side-effects. Then Becky's husband, Henry, was killed in a car accident. She's had to work incredibly hard to keep the shop going, and I know that she doesn't always get to spend as much time with David as she wants to. So the local trading association set up the charity. It helps fund someone to help out in the shop for extra shifts, and for Becky and David to do fun things together, like visiting Disneyland Paris last summer. The whole town has pitched in with different fundraisers, and we're really going for it this Christmas because he's due to have an operation that will mean Becky taking a lot of time off work.'

'You don't get a sense of community like that in many places these days.' Even as he spoke, the irony of Ben's own words wasn't lost on him. It was true, though. At least it would be great for lots of people, even if it would be hell on earth for someone like him.

'The way people have pulled together to help two of their own is one of the reasons I like living here so much.' She led him towards the till area, and he realised he was holding *five* books. She really was good at this.

'I guess I'd better grab my chance and look at that house, then.' Ben took a pen off the counter and scribbled his number onto the back of a flyer advertising a craft fair. 'Maybe you could pass this on for me, ask your contact if she'd be comfortable with me going to take a look?'

'Perhaps it would be better if I took you round there myself.' Her eyes met his and he was shocked by how much he liked the sound of that offer. 'If you're sure you can spare the time, that would be great.'

'I'll ring Sarah-Jane and text you later to confirm the details.' Smiling, she rang up the last of his purchases, and he handed over his credit card — hardly even registering that he'd just spent over fifty pounds on books for a child he barely knew.

4

Maddie shook herself. Had she really offered to accompany Ben to view Sarah-Jane's cottage? Now that she was about to meet him to take him up there, she was seriously having second thoughts. He must think she was really pushy — or, worse still, just some lonely shop assistant desperate for a date. Either way, the thought made her cheeks flame with colour. It had been so long since someone had walked into her shop or her life that she'd felt such an instant connection to . . . perhaps it was no surprise she'd acted in a way that had surprised even her.

Glancing in the mirror of the small bathroom for customers and staff at the back of the shop, she sighed. There was no time to change — her usual uniform of jeans and white cotton shirt would have to do. Cecil's Adventures was her *raison d'être*, and she'd never resented the long hours she'd to put in, but it had left almost no time for anything else during the past three years.

Just ten minutes after she'd finally put up the CLOSED sign on the door, there was a knock on the glass. Praying it would be Ben, rather than a customer hoping for some out-of-hours shopping, she sprayed a quick spritz of perfume and walked through to the front of shop.

He was leaning on the glass, peering in, his outline illuminated by the streetlight outside the shop. Tall and muscular, he didn't look as though he spent all day surveying properties — more as if he built them, with powerful shoulders, and . . . Opening the door of the shop, the cool night air enveloped her as she pulled on her jacket. Hopefully the cold would help bring her back to her senses. Something had to.

'You got my text, then?' She could have kicked herself for the stupid question. Why else would he be here if he hadn't got it?

'I tried to reply, but the mobile signal at The Quill and Ink is, how shall I put it, interesting!' He smiled in a way that lit up his eyes. 'I leant out of the bedroom window, even stood on one leg, but it still wouldn't go through.'

'It is pretty appalling in parts of the Bay, and inside that old building it's almost impossible to get a signal, I should think. It's almost like it's clinging onto its own history and refusing to accept modern technology. Maureen, the landlady, told me once that guests sometimes have to walk up to the clifftops just to get their phones to work. Still, she seems to do okay, and people come back year after year. There are other compensations, I suspect.'

'It's certainly a great-looking old building.' He spoke as they walked back past the coaching inn towards Sarah-Jane's cottage. 'I read something in the guestbook about Maureen's legendary fry-ups, so I'm assuming they're a major draw, too. Although I haven't had the chance to try one yet.'

'Well, I can vouch for them!' Maddie felt hungry just thinking about it. 'Once a month, Rosie and I treat ourselves to a Sunday morning special there. Only not this month, as I've been opening seven days a week in the run up to Christmas.'

'It's a big commitment, this business of yours; it can't leave much time for anything else?' Ben was echoing Maddie's thoughts from earlier, but she shrugged, not wanting to admit just how hard it sometimes was doing it all on her own. 'No-one special to help you out with it all, then, or any family?'

'No, it's just me and Enid most of the time; but she doesn't work weekends because of her own family, so I've got the Henderson twins who help me out on Saturdays. They're seventeen, and not that interested in the books, but they work hard and the tearoom is always busy with teenage girls at the weekends — at least partly because of them. Sometimes I get a bit of extra casual help in, but my family live down in Cornwall, and there's no partner — business or otherwise.' Warmth flooded her cheeks again, and she wondered if that had sounded as awkward as it felt.

'My gain, then, or otherwise I don't think you'd be up for accompanying me to look at this cottage tonight.' He sounded relieved, although he didn't seem the sort of man who found it hard to make a decision on his own.

'How about you? Is there someone you'll need to call to come and see the cottage, if you think it might be suitable?' She knew he wasn't married from the way he'd answered Rosie's questions earlier. But trying to find out more without sounding obvious was proving tricky. She had no idea how to do this sort of thing any more: it had been so long.

'No, everyone in my family says I work far too hard for that.' There was a note of something in his voice, something she couldn't quite pin down, but it was clear he didn't agree. 'So it's just me to please, which is why I could do with a second opinion.'

They made their way further up the high street, which was strung from side to side with lights, each depicting a scene from *A Christmas Carol*.

'We just need to take this road on the left.' Love Lane led down towards the river, just to the left of the only bridge that served a single road in and out of town, unless you wanted to take a huge detour via the Welham Valley, or come in by sea. Sarah-Jane's cottage was what an estate agent would undoubtedly call 'chocolate-box'. It was double-fronted, with a thatched roof, and small lead-light windows offering a view of the river. Maddie had always loved it, and if Ben wasn't a fan, then there was no hope for him in a place like St Nicholas Bay.

'Is this it?' For a second she thought there were tears in his eyes, but she had to be imagining it, because he smiled again almost instantly. 'I saw it on the way in. It's gorgeous, and if I took this place on, my mother would think all her Christmases had come at once. She's always telling me I should get a permanent base, and this is exactly like the house Will and I were born in.'

'Does your mum still live there?'

'No, we moved out when I was twelve and Will was only six. She really missed the place, though; we all did.' The look on his face said there was more to the story, but she didn't want to push him. He'd tell her if he wanted to.

'Shall we take a look inside then?' Maddie gestured towards Sarah-Jane's cottage; Ben nodded absently, as though he was lost in his own thoughts.

The cottage had a red front door with a shiny brass knocker in the middle, which made a satisfying thud as it knocked against the wood.

'Maddie!' Answering the door, Sarah-Jane greeted them enthusiastically, her blonde hair immaculately swept up into a neat chignon and her perfume seeming to cling to the air around her. She was wearing a fitted pale-grey woollen dress, and make-up that looked like it had been done by a professional. Maddie instantly felt scruffy in comparison, and tucked her dark hair behind her ears, as though that might make a difference. 'And you must be Ben?' Sarah-Jane held out her hand, her nails and jewellery matching the rest of her — classy and expensive-looking. If Maddie hadn't known she worked full time and had two children, she might have cut herself a break; but Sarah-Jane was just one of those people who really did seem to have it all.

'Nice to meet you and thanks for letting us come around like this.' Ben shook her hand. 'I gather a property coming up for rent in St Nicholas Bay is about as rare as hen's teeth?'

'It's no trouble at all.' Stepping back, Sarah-Jane ushered her inside the house, which was warm and cosy in only the way a house with such a low ceiling could be. Maddie noticed Ben having to duck his head a couple of times — to avoid the oak beams — but it didn't seem to bother him. 'I'll show you around whilst Andrew makes us all a drink.'

The house was lovely, but not decorated in entirely the way Maddie would have. Each room was perfect, as though Sarah-Jane had lifted the contents from a glossy magazine or a Cath Kidston shop, so it seemed more like a show home than a family home as a result. The decoration was beautiful, but lacked any real personal touches — and, given that Sarah-Jane had two young children, her fridge was distinctly lacking in childish paintings haphazardly attached with handmade *I Love Mum* magnets.

'So, what do you think?' Sarah-Jane asked as her husband Andrew busied himself making their drinks. 'Do I need to contact an agent, or might we have a deal?'

'It's great.' Taking the coffee that Andrew handed him, Ben nodded.

'We'll have to talk money at some point, of course, and what your lease agreement would look like, but I'm definitely interested.'

'Fantastic!' Sarah-Jane smiled, clapping her hands together. 'Andrew works from home as a conveyancer in between doing all the childcare stuff, so I'm sure the two of you can thrash out all the details. I'm being seconded to Dubai for a couple of years, and we'll be using the London flat when we come back to visit, so you could have the place for the whole time if you wanted to?'

'It's usual to do six months at a time, darling,' Andrew interjected, his eyes flickering from Maddie to Ben as if looking for some support. 'But I'm sure Ben and I can sort out the details, as you say.'

'Fine, fine, you know I'm happy to leave all of that to you. But perhaps we should forget the wine and have something a bit stronger to celebrate?'

* * *

61

It was past nine o'clock before Ben and Maddie had managed to extricate themselves from Sarah-Jane's kitchen. He'd wanted to ask if Maddie fancied joining him for dinner at The Quill and Ink, but he suspected they would already have stopped serving food. There were a couple of takeaway restaurants they'd passed on their way up to Sarah-Jane's place, though he would much prefer to sit across a table from Maddie and talk to her some more — so eating a portion of fish and chips straight from the paper wasn't ideal.

'Is there anywhere we can still get a meal at this time of the evening?' Perhaps he was being presumptuous — she might well have plans for the evening — but he of all people knew that you didn't get if you didn't ask.

'Well, I'm pretty sure that Martha's Tavernita serves food until ten p.m. in December: Sebastian asked me to put some flyers in the tearoom to advertise the extended hours.' Maddie turned towards him and, for the first time, he noticed what looked like tiny flecks of gold in her green eyes. 'They serve tapas, and the most fantastic halloumi and chorizo kebabs in the world.'

'Sounds fantastic. I thought we'd be stuck with some sort of takeaway at this time of night, but tapas would be great. I take it that 'Martha's' is another Dickens reference?' He couldn't really justify spending this much time with a potential client from a business perspective — if anything, getting too close could cloud his judgement. He liked Maddie, though, and it had nothing to do with her owning the lease to a prime commercial property. There were definitely worse ways to spend an evening.

'Martha was the name of Bob Cratchit's eldest daughter in the book. I suspect Tiny Tim's Tavernita would have been their first choice for the alliteration, but Meg at the toy shop had already taken that one. In fact, I'm a bit of a rebel in these parts, not giving my shop a name with any connection to the story. I named my shop for much more personal reasons, and they mean more to me than giving Dickens yet another nod.'

Ben didn't respond. Whatever her reasons for naming the shop, this wasn't the ideal thing to hear when you were hoping to persuade someone that even sentiment had its price.

Martha's Tavernita was half-way back down the high street towards Cecil's Adventures, and the window was decorated with a hand-painted scene from *A Christmas Carol*. The characters were standing next to a huge poinsettia rather than a Christmas tree, making it somehow distinctly Spanish in theme. Ben smiled to himself. This town certainly knew how to work their alleged associations with Dickens' Christmas story, and he could already picture the themed décor of the Hemmingway's they'd be opening in St Nicholas Bay, if all went according to plan. They were unlikely to be as rebellious as Maddie about naming it, either.

'Ah, Madeleina, so good to see you!' A man, who Ben assumed was the restaurant owner, came out from behind the bar in one corner and kissed Maddie on both cheeks.

'Good to see you too, Sebastian. But the question is, can you fit us in without a reservation?' As Maddie spoke, she looked as though she was scanning the restaurant for a likely spot. It certainly seemed popular, and the smell of garlic and chilli made Ben realise how hungry he really was.

'For you, Madeleina, I will find a table or throw someone else out!' Sebastian smiled and leant conspiratorially towards her, so that Ben had to strain to hear what he said. 'And have you taken care of Maria's present for me? You know I'm relying on you!'

'All sorted; it should be here by Monday.'

'Thank you, Bonita, in which case I'll give you some wine on the house.'

Sebastian's eyes swept over her, and Ben recognised that look. Whoever Maria was, he clearly wasn't entirely devoted to her. 'Give me a moment and I'll have a table ready for you.'

Within seconds, Sebastian had set a table for them by the window, and by the time they sat down he was already uncorking a bottle of Rioja.

'Thanks, Sebastian. Can I introduce you to my friend Ben? He's thinking of renting Sarah-Jane's place whilst she's in Dubai.' Maddie smoothed her napkin and Sebastian gave a curt nod, barely disguising his disinterest, before handing them both a menu and moving on to another table to take their order.

'Who's Maria?' Ben glanced the menu as he spoke. For some reason, it mattered to him more than it should that Maddie seemed so close to the restaurant owner.

'She's Sebastian's sister, and the chef here.' Maddie looked up from her menu at the same time as he did, and their eyes met for a moment. She was beautiful, all the more so because she didn't play on it. 'She wanted a rare Spanish cookbook from 1901, called *El Rey de los Cocineros*, and I managed to track down a copy from a dealer in the States.'

'You really do offer a personal service, don't you?' He was looking for some reassurance that what she'd done for Sebastian was nothing special; although it would have been better for the potential purchase of the lease if Maddie wasn't dealing in books. That certainly wasn't a service that Hemmingway's would offer. If it wasn't instant and downloadable, then it wasn't for them.

'I've found over the three years I've been running the shop that there are all sorts of things I can diversify into that have helped make it a success.' Her eyes shone when she spoke about her work, and he didn't have to probe to get the information he needed. 'I started doing a lot of community things — like meet-ups for mothers and toddlers, book groups, that sort of thing. The cakes and refreshments just started off as an added extra, but combining the books with a tearoom seems to have given me a bit of a unique edge.' She laughed. 'In fact, my high school business studies tutor would be amazed: I actually must have listened accidentally once or twice when he was talking about Unique Selling Points. Whatever it was, it's led to other stuff, like the gingerbread party you saw earlier. And we do kids' birthday parties and have readings by authors. I started doing some finding, and a bit of dealing, in rare books and first editions, too. People just don't seem to have the time to dedicate to the research to track them down themselves, and it's proved a fairly lucrative little sideline.'

'How do you find the time, what with working so many hours in the shop?' Part of him was dreading the answer; and, when it came, it confirmed what he'd feared.

'I suppose because I don't worry about a work-life balance like other people do. I love Cecil's Adventures and I love books, so when your work is your passion you don't feel like you need a break from it.' She closed her menu and took a sip of the Rioja. 'What about you — are you passionate about your work?'

'I suppose I'm passionate about it in a way. Sealing the deal is what's most important to me.' Although he wasn't being entirely open, he didn't want to lie to her, either. 'But if you're asking whether I grew up dreaming of leasing commercial properties, then the answer would have to be no.'

'What did you dream about doing back then?' Maddie fixed him with that intense look she had: the one that made him want to tell her everything, things he'd barely thought about for years. Being in St Nicholas Bay had been a strange experience: the cottage that had reminded him so much of his childhood home, the things in Tiny Tim's Toys,

69

and meeting someone like Maddie, had all brought back memories — some of which he'd rather have kept buried. Thankfully, Sebastian interrupted when he came to take their order; and, by the time he'd gone, Ben had managed to swallow his confession.

'So, I was asking you what it was you wanted to do when you were a child?' Maddie smiled again and he tried not to think about what it would be like to kiss her.

'Oh, you know. The usual stuff, I expect; become a train driver or a pilot, something like that.' He took a slug of his wine as an image of the handmade wooden castle in the boot of his car flitted into his mind. It was intended for his niece, something personal from an uncle that never had time to visit, and it was far more meaningful than the party dress that now sat beside it.

'So why didn't you follow your dream?' As Maddie spoke, he reached to pour her another glass of wine, and wrestled with exactly how much to reveal.

'Circumstances.' The hostel that he sometimes still dreamt about in the dead of night wasn't easy to erase from his thoughts. His mother's exhausted face, pale and drawn, Will sobbing, and them clutching on to a few black bin bags containing all they owned was still the stuff of nightmares. But Ben had got them out of there and, at the age of twelve, had to be stronger than many grown men could have been in the same circumstances. He was proud of that and knew it had made him the man he'd become. His mother would say those same words, about how quickly he'd grown up, with a look of sadness on her face that he couldn't quite come to terms with. 'I had to get a job when my father died. I guess I didn't have time to daydream about the things that other boys of that age do, but everyone said even back then that I could sell ice to Eskimos. So, in a weird kind of way, I guess I found my true vocation by accident.'

'It must have been hard, having those choices taken away from you, and losing your dad at the same time.' Maddie's voice was like warm honey and he could have listened to it all night. Even if she was asking questions that he didn't really want to answer.

'I suppose it was, but I got by, and I think it was harder still on my mum and Will. He barely has any memories of Dad.' He didn't add that his father's death had just been the catalyst to set a house of cards coming crashing down around them. Maybe it was pride, but whatever it was it wasn't something he was going to talk about. 'So, what about you? Did you *always* dream of owning a bookshop? You're quite young to have set up on your own.'

'I was lucky.' Maddie smiled again, but there was a definite sadness in her eyes. 'I had the most wonderful grandfather, who gave me a love for books that opened up a whole world of adventures for me; and when he died, he left me enough money to set up the shop.'

'Was his name Cecil, by any chance?' Ben swallowed another mouthful of wine, which tasted suddenly bitter.

'It was and he was wonderful. I'd never tell my parents, of course, but in many ways I think he was the biggest influence in my life. He died at Christmas, five years ago, and so I always think about him more at this time of year than at any other, but it's starting to get easier and I can remember the good times more than the end now. I expect it's the same with your Dad, but it takes a while, doesn't it?'

Ben nodded, but he didn't speak. He didn't want to tell her that almost twenty years later it was still virtually impossible for him to recall the good times. So he was relieved when they were interrupted again, this time by Sebastian bringing over the first of their dishes of tapas.

'Here we go, Benita, your favourite.'

He set down a brown earthenware dish with skewers of haloumi and chorizo heaped upon it. 'I'll be sure to make an extra plateful for David's fundraiser.'

'That would be great, Sebastian; you're a star.' Maddie gave their host another one of the smiles which lit up her whole face. She had a dimple on one side, which made Ben want to see her smile all the more. 'We've sold nearly all the tickets, so Becky should be able to get him whatever he wants for Christmas, and take him somewhere wonderful for a break next year. Hopefully her shop will get a bit quieter in January, and the rest of us can rally round so they can go off for a bit of sun.'

'Ah, *sun*.' Sebastian looked wistful. 'Don't you ever think of leaving these cold grey shores and heading somewhere hot, like Spain? I can see you there, Madeleina; you could come out and run a restaurant with me, your cakes are almost as good as my alfores.' He winked, and Ben had to admire the other man's bravado. Here they were, to all intents and purposes, on a date, and Sebastian was trying to persuade Maddie to elope with him — even if he was saying it in a way that made it hard to tell if he was joking.

'No, I never want to leave. I love it here.' Maddie's words prickled the skin on the back of Ben's neck. 'If you even thought about it, Maria would hunt you down with her best carving knife. And as for your mother . . . '

'I know, I know, or else I'd be out there now — sitting in the sun somewhere, waiting to celebrate Pascuas — but instead, I'll just dream.' Sebastian shrugged his shoulders in a typically Latin gesture. 'Enjoy your meal, Benita.'

'So, what's this fundraiser, then?' Ben picked up one of the skewers that Maddie had been so keen for him to try. She was right, it was the food of the Gods — the warm cheese and spicy sausages danced across his tastebuds.

'It's for our friend Becky Moore. She

was widowed two years ago and she's bringing up her little boy, David, on her own. I showed you the poster in the shop.'

'Oh, yes, I remember. Is there anything I could do to help out?' He already had an idea — a way that Hemmingway's might get a foothold in the local community's affections, which might help when the time came to reveal their intentions. But for now, they would have to keep quiet about any involvement. They didn't need a protest march on their hands.

'You could buy one of the last tickets, if you're still around. We're having a quiz in Cecil's Adventures next weekend, and an auction of promises, so maybe you could offer us something for that?' She raised an eyebrow, and there was a slight twitch at the corner of her lips. If he'd doubted their attraction was mutual, he knew it was now.

'I'll certainly buy a ticket, and I can do better than offering a promise. The company I work for does something called 'matched funding' for worthwhile causes, so if I can get their agreement, they'll double whatever you raise for David on the night.' Ben grinned at the delight that spread across Maddie's face.

'That's brilliant!' She leant across the table. 'But are you sure you're still going to be around? I don't think you'll find anywhere nicer that Sarah-Jane's place to rent, but I guess you've got other things lined up to look at?'

'I'm going to look at a couple of commercial premises on the other side of the Welham Valley, and a few in Canterbury, so I've booked to stay at The Quill and Ink until the twenty-third.' Ben was planning to have the deal signed and sealed by then. He had a feeling that Maddie wouldn't be keen to spend much time with him when she found out who he worked for, so he wanted to make the most of it. In the meantime, he could press on and agree the details with Andrew to rent his and

Sarah-Jane's property, so long as they'd agree to add a sub-letting clause. He doubted, given the sense of community in St Nicholas Bay, that they'd welcome him back with open arms once they found out what Hemmingway's had planned . . . but it would make a perfect home for Will and his family. His little brother still felt like his responsibility, even though he now had a daughter of his own. He wanted Will out of the dingy flat he was living in, and St Nicholas Bay was an ideal place to raise a child.

'I'm really pleased you're staying on for a while, and it's great that you can do something so wonderful for David while you're here.' Maddie put her hand on his. 'I don't think you've ever said who it is you work for?'

'It's just a catering company who are always on the lookout for suitable commercial premises; nothing that's going to set the world alight.' It was still a half-truth, but it was the closest he'd come to lying to her, and it felt surprisingly uncomfortable. If he mentioned Hemmingway's, though, she'd know exactly who they were. A chain of coffee shops which would be the death knell to a little independent business like hers. Not only that, but they offered free e-book downloads with every purchase and a wifi connection that would be three times faster than the average, meaning they would be in direct competition with somewhere like Cecil's Adventures; maybe without the personal touch, but with a technical edge and massive investment behind them. She'd never be able to compete, especially as Hemmingway's had recently diversified into being licensed premises after seven pm, so they'd be able to offer Maddie's book groups and other community events a bottle of wine with their free downloads.

'Maybe not, but at least they sound generous. I can't wait to see David's little face when he gets everything on his Christmas list.' Maddie touched his hand again, and he almost wished he still believed in the magic of Christmas. Sadly, he'd stopped believing in anything but making your own luck years before.

5

The week leading up to David's fundraiser had been a frantically busy one for Maddie. The shop had thronged with tourists, and she'd sold more copies of *A Christmas Carol* in one week than she had in the rest of the year, even though it always retailed pretty well. There'd been a queue back past her shop window to get into Ebenezer's Christmas Emporium, so she knew Becky and her staff would have been rushed off their feet too. Although her friend's shop ticked over for the whole year, because of the town's association with Christmas and the tourists' willingness to buy ornaments to remember their visit by, it relied on the annual December trade to keep in the black over the next eleven months.

'Can I do anything for tonight?'

Becky looked exhausted, the last run-up to Christmas was clearly taking its toll. It was just after six pm, and, like Maddie, she'd only just shut up shop for the day.

'It's all in hand, Becky, honestly.' Maddie passed her a chocolate-covered biscuit in the shape of a Christmas tree. 'Take this for a quick energy boost, and then go and see that gorgeous boy of yours for a bit before it all gets started here.'

'I feel really bad, leaving it all to you while I just swan off.' To hear Becky speak, anyone would have thought she was going off to do something completely frivolous. As wonderful as David was, Maddie knew he could be demanding when he had his mum to himself. And the rest of the time, Becky was working to provide for them and pay the childminder who picked him up from school and looked after him whilst she was working. As relentless as the hours in her own shop sometimes seemed, Maddie was well aware she had it easy in comparison.

'I've told you, it's all fine.' She smiled and gently placed her hand in the small of her friend's back. If she had to force her out of the shop, she would. 'Rosie said she'd be here by half six, Kate's coming too, and I think there might be one or two others coming over to help me set up as well.' Almost as soon as the words were out of her mouth, the door of the shop pinged again and Ben was framed in the doorway.

He looked great as always, wearing black jeans and a charcoal-grey jumper with a black jacket over the top. As he opened the door, he brought the cold in with him, making her shiver. They'd managed one lunch date at The Quill and Ink — although Enid had then phoned to say there'd been a mix-up on one of the orders, and that the delivery driver was demanding to see the manager before he'd take the books back. Maddie had left in the middle of dessert, but even missing out on warm chocolate-and-walnut brownies wasn't as disappointing as not getting to spend some more time with Ben. There was something different about him; he was intelligent and funny, but there were some hidden depths in his past that he didn't seem quite ready to share.

For the rest of the time, she'd either been too busy or he had. There'd been the book club's Christmas party, and a reading by a local author who'd written a series of Christmas stories on another evening, and then a children's author on a third night; and she'd babysat for Becky on the Thursday so she could go late-night shopping in Canterbury for some of David's presents. Ben had been busy most days with the viewings he'd booked in; and, on the only other evening, Maddie had a long-standing arrangement to go out with Rosie for a pre-Christmas drink. It had felt a bit like fate was standing in their way. He was here now, though, and suddenly she was keener than ever to get Becky to go home before Rosie arrived . . . only her feelings weren't altogether altruistic this time around.

'Becky, this is Ben — he's the friend I told you about who's managed to get some matched funding for tonight.' Maddie moved aside as Becky clasped his hand.

'Thanks so much, I've heard such a lot about you!' Becky was gushing and making it sound as though Maddie hadn't stopped talking about him. She might have mentioned him once or twice over the pot of coffee they'd shared when she'd gone round to babysit David, but surely she hadn't been too obvious. Had she?

'You're more than welcome. It's nothing, really; just a phone call to the right person. Anyway, how could I resist after seeing a picture of David?' Ben smiled, and Maddie found herself hoping there wasn't too much bad news lurking in those hidden depths of his.

'You can stop worrying about what there is to do now, Becky. Ben can help me start setting up and, once Rosie and Kate get here, we'll have it all finished before you know it. I've baked enough cakes and biscuits to feed an army, and Sebastian is bringing down a load of savoury stuff. So, honestly, there's nothing you need to do.'

'Okay, okay, I get the message. And I do need all the time I can get to make myself look half-decent!' Kissing Maddie on both cheeks, she headed for the door. 'I'll see you both later, then; and thanks again, Ben, it really means a lot.'

'I can see why you wanted to help her.' Ben followed Maddie towards the far end of the shop, after Becky had left. 'She's lovely.'

'Yes, she is.' She slid the flipchart stand that they were going to use for the quiz out from behind one of the bookcases. 'And if you don't love David, then we might just have to arrange for three ghosts to visit you and remind you what it's like to be human.'

'Now you sound just like my mum.' He was smiling, but his voice was flat, and she immediately regretted the comment. 'She'd love your décor, too.'

Maddie had placed an eight-foot Christmas tree in one corner of the shop, decorated with figurines from *A Christmas Carol* and characters from other classic Christmas stories. She'd also spent hours making bunting from reproduction book covers of Christmas-themed stories. There were fairy lights strung from every bookcase, and if it was over the top, she didn't care — she loved it, and so did her customers.

'Christmas is what we do in St Nicholas Bay.'

'I meant it — she'd adore it, and even an old Grinch like me can see that.' Ben laughed, and this time it was genuine. 'In fact, I can see you've got my likeness on the tree!' He gestured towards the green Dr Seuss character hanging on one of the higher branches.

'Don't you like Christmas, then?' Maddie studied him from a moment. The fact that he was anything but an open book — perhaps the ultimate irony for someone in her line of work — made him all the more interesting.

Yet, each time they met, it was as though she'd managed to strip another layer away.

'I don't dislike it as such. It frustrates me that half the business world seems to shut down for about two weeks, but my place only shuts down for the mandatory bank holidays. If liking it that way makes me a Grinch, then I guess I am.'

'You know you have to refer to yourself as a Scrooge around here, don't you? No other maligner of Christmas will do.' She lifted up two of the beanbags from the bookshop area of the store and carried them towards the tearoom, Ben following her lead. 'Although, given that you've been responsible for doubling the fundraising tonight, I suppose we can't call you that. Have you got plans for the big day?'

'Nothing set in stone.' He stacked the beanbags on top of the ones she'd just set down, and their eyes met for a moment. 'How about you?'

'I've had a couple of invitations. At the moment, it's a toss-up between joining Rosie's family, whose mum makes the best Christmas dinner in the world; or spending it with Becky and David. Even over the offer of great food, I think seeing David's face on Christmas morning will win.' Maddie walked behind the counter to the kitchen area of the tearoom and came back with two punch glasses, the smell of cinnamon and cloves filling the air around her. 'Do you have any objections to Christmas punch?'

'None at all!' He took a glass from her and they carried them through to the other end of the shop, chatting easily whilst they moved all of the beanbags and easy chairs from the bookshop to one end of the tearoom, making it look as if removal men might arrive any minute. By the time they'd finished arranging the tables and chairs in the space left behind, there was enough room for the quiz teams to fight it out for first place.

'Another glass?' When they'd finally got everything ready, and there was still no sign of Rosie or Kate, Maddie went back behind the counter to top up their drinks. As she passed him his glass back, their hands touched — just like they had in Martha's Tavernita — and she felt the same jolt of recognition she'd noticed that night. She was attracted to him, no doubt about it. It was something which didn't happen often these days — but she was a grown-up, not a schoolgirl. It was Christmas, and if she wanted to kiss him, then there was nothing to stop her from letting him know.

Leaning forward, he mirrored her movement, kissing her softly on the mouth. Pulling away for a moment, he took her glass and set it next to his on the counter, before linking his arms around her waist and pulling her towards him. The second kiss left her in no doubt — the attraction was definitely mutual. But the sound of his head making contact with something, and a muffled curse as he pulled away from her again, broke the spell.

'What on earth was that thing?' Ben swung round and reached up towards the offending object: a heavy wooden model of a biplane, complete with a wooden pilot sporting a leather helmet with earflaps and goggles, suspended from the ceiling by a metal cord. It hung on the staff side of the counter and was too high up to affect Maddie or Enid; but, as she'd leant against Ben's chest, it had struck him on the side of the head.

'It's *Cecil's Adventure*.' Maddie looked up at the wooden figure in the plane as she spoke. It was a silly thing to think, but it was almost as if it was trying to tell her something. 'When I saw it in a second-hand shop in Canterbury, it reminded me so much of the stories my granddad used to tell about seeing the world on his adventures, that I just has to buy it. It was all make-believe, of course, but now I like to think of him like that — still flying off on adventures wherever he is. I use the image on all my menus and on the website. I'm sorry he hit you, though — he's never done that before!'

'I'll try not to take it personally.' Ben grinned. 'Now, where were we . . . ?'

As he took a step towards her, the bell on the shop doorway pinged again and Rosie, looking like an explosion in a Christmas decoration factory, finally arrived — with Kate in tow.

Maddie wasn't sure why, but she felt like throwing her arms around her friends. She liked Ben, but something was making her nervous about how fast things were moving. Maybe it was just because her last relationship had finished before she'd even opened the shop, or perhaps it was because there was no guarantee Ben would stick around if he didn't decide to rent Sarah-Jane's place. Whatever it was, it felt like Rosie and Kate had saved her from something.

'Ben, this is Kate, she teaches at the local primary school.' Maddie concentrated on keeping her tone light. 'And, of course, you've met Rosie before.'

'Great to meet you, Ben. I've heard all about you from Rosie!' Kate held out her hand and smiled as Ben shook it.

'You too, but if Rosie's given you the low-down, I won't even try to defend myself!'

'You look amazing!' Maddie stopped fighting the urge to give Rosie a hug and found herself pushed up against acres of scratchy sequins and tinsel as she did so. Rosie was dressed a bit like a disco ball, with a skin-tight silver-sequinned dress. She had three boas of tinsel strung over her shoulders in silver and purple, and huge earrings in the shape of Christmas baubles, as well as a tiara that bore the message *Merry Christmas* spelled out in different-coloured diamantes. As she always did, Maddie felt gloriously underdressed next to her friend. Although Kate was looking equally overwhelmed by Rosie's flamboyance.

'She does look great, doesn't she?'

Kate gave Maddie a rueful grin. 'I wish I'd worn something other than my teacher's weekend uniform of jeans and a jumper — although I could never hold a candle to Rosie.'

'You always look fab. It's me who must look like I've been dragged through a hedge backwards!' Maddie smoothed her hair, her face still flushed from the kiss and the confusion of emotions she'd felt as a result.

'Of course you don't, and you wouldn't be so harassed anyway if I'd got here on time and not spent so long getting ready.' Rosie grinned as she gave Maddie the back-handed compliment — not knowing how accurate her words were. 'I know the outfit's over the top, but I love Christmas almost as much as I love little David, and I couldn't stop adding the bling once I got started.' She helped herself to a glass of punch, the smell of Christmas filling the air once again.

'Perfectly justifiable being late, to make an entrance like that. You look the queen of Christmas in that outfit.' Ben gave Rosie a mock bow. Perhaps he'd been as relived as Maddie that they'd been interrupted.

'It's great to see you again, Ben. Merry almost Christmas.' Rosie kissed him enthusiastically on both cheeks. 'Although there's still plenty of time to pop into my shop and get that little niece of yours another present or two, you know?'

'I might just take you up on that. In the meantime, is there anything left to do before the others arrive, Maddie?' He turned to look at her, and she couldn't quite meet his gaze. She might have made the first move, but it really did feel like being a schoolgirl all over again. In books, it was always much easier than this — especially the sort that Rosie loved so much. But then, Maddie had always had a habit of reading the last chapter before she'd even started a book, so she knew how it would all turn out — she couldn't relax otherwise. Only real life didn't afford that opportunity, which she'd often thought was probably just as well, or she might never start anything — least of all a new relationship.

'We're pretty much done. I just hope enough people turn up to make it worthwhile.' She crossed her fingers. Everyone had gone to so much effort, and now Ben was going to double the money raised, so she desperately didn't want to let Becky and David down. The little boy was on a waiting list for an operation to loosen the muscles that had tightened around his hips following the meningitis, and Becky would need to have a lot of time away from the shop when the time came. So they were hoping to raise enough money to both give him a Christmas to remember, and make sure that the months ahead were as stress-free for his mum as they possibly could be.

'It'll be great!' Rosie gave a twirl and flicked one of the tinsel boas over her shoulder. 'After all, I'm going to be your lovely assistant whilst you're reading out the quiz questions and taking the auction bids, and who could resist me in this outfit?!' She burst into infectious laughter, and some of the tension left Maddie's shoulders. It was going to be a good night, and she had to stop worrying about things before they'd even happened — which included fretting over what might happen next with Ben. He was a visitor to St Nicholas Bay, and would be gone by Christmas. So, worrying — as her grandfather's favourite quote went — was like walking around with an umbrella up, waiting for it to rain.

*　*　*

As it turned out, Maddie's apprehension was completely pointless, because the evening went brilliantly. Although there were no surprises when she added up the scores.

'The winning team are St. Nicholas Bay Juniors!' She lifted a small hamper of wine and chocolate off the table where she and Rosie had been sitting to host the quiz. Kate and some of the other staff from the school, along with a few of their friends, made up the winning team. When she made the announcement, they whooped with such enthusiasm that anyone would have thought they'd just broken a world record.

'Congratulations!' Handing over the prize, Maddie looked at the piece of paper Rosie had just pushed towards her, a lump forming in her throat as she did so.

'Are you sure this is right?' she whispered to Rosie, who nodded, her broad smile offering further confirmation.

She could still barely believe it. There'd been six teams of eight squeezed into the shop in the end, and they'd all become extremely generous by the time the auction came round at the mid-way break in the quiz — due in no small part to the potency of the Christmas punch. Even so, raising fifteen hundred pounds was more than she could ever have believed they would. With the matched funding from Ben's firm, that meant there'd be three thousand pounds to top up the coffers of 'Dreams for David'.

Ben was still being elusive about the name of his company — something about them not wanting publicity for charitable donations — but she was determined to find out in the end. They needed to know just what sort of difference their gesture was making to the lives of two really special people.

However, that was something to sort out another day. Right now, she had an important announcement to make.

'There's one more thing I'd like to say before you all head off tonight.' Maddie swallowed hard. Looking at the faces around her, the people who had welcomed her with such warmth into their home town, and who were here tonight to support Becky and her little boy, made her suddenly emotional. 'I just wanted to thank you all for coming tonight, so close to Christmas when you've all got so much on. And for being so generous with donations of prizes and auction bids. I'm delighted to tell you that we've raised almost fifteen hundred pounds, and with the matched funding secured by Ben's company, that means we can add three thousand pounds to David's trust.'

The cheering in the room eclipsed the winning team's celebrations by some margin. They were all winners. Becky made her way to the front of the room, folding Maddie into a hug that left them both breathless.

'Can I say a few words?' Becky's voice was shaking slightly, and her hands even more so as she took the mike from Maddie.

'I can't even begin to thank you all.' She turned to look at Maddie, the rest of the room falling silent. 'Especially this wonderful woman and her band of helpers who made everything possible tonight. And, of course, to Ben for doubling the money.' Becky held up her hand when they both started to protest. 'I know you'll all say it's nothing, but it really isn't. I'm crying right now, but they're happy tears, I promise you. When Henry died, it was so unexpected, and we hadn't properly planned in case anything like that happened. If I wanted to stay in the Bay, I knew I had to somehow keep the shop going, but I didn't know how I'd do that and manage to spend enough time with David. My parents have him tonight, but it's only because they're down for the weekend; and, much as they'd love to help me more, there's not that much they can do when they live two hours' drive away. So when I lost Henry, my choice was between moving there, or staying here and somehow trying to do the impossible — keep a business and a family going all by myself.' Becky paused, and Maddie briefly caught Ben's eye, trying to read the expression there, but he quickly dropped his gaze. 'Only I wasn't by myself. Everyone rallied round and made life for the two of us worth living again. If I ever think I've been unlucky losing Henry like that, I remember where I live and the friends I've got around me.'

Becky put down the mike and made her way back to her seat. With everyone cheering even louder than before, Maddie turned to look at Ben again. He'd disappeared, gone without saying a word. It felt as if her blood was running cold. She barely knew him. What if he'd invented the story about matching the funding? She'd told Becky — and a packed room of her friends and neighbours — that the money raised had been doubled. Maybe she'd built up Becky's hopes about how much they'd raised for nothing, a sham.

*   *   *

Ben closed the door of Cecil's Adventures behind him, the cheering still ringing in his ears. He hadn't expected to feel like this. After all, he'd just helped double the money Maddie and her friends had raised. But he hadn't been honest with her; and, the more he got to know her, the more he was convinced she'd hate Hemmingway's. In every negotiation, it was always a question of finding the right moment to reveal who he worked for, which was usually after the first offer was made. It wasn't as if it was unethical; he knew other chains who used acquisition agents, and kept their name out of it until it was too late for the seller to pull out. Yet he still felt guilty. He needed to get on with securing the lease to Rosie's shop and the sub-letting of the cottage. There was no way he'd talk Maddie into letting go of her shop, even if he was honest with her. But once Hemmingway's opened next door, it would only be a matter of time before Cecil's Adventures went under, and he had to try to find a way of convincing her that there really was only one choice.

What was right for Hemmingway's was beginning to feel wrong in every other way. But he couldn't afford to let sentiment cloud his judgement — that was the way to ruin, and he had the emotional scars to prove it.

6

Maddie looked at the stacks of books again. There should definitely be enough, and they'd been sorted into age and gender categories. She'd added about ten more to the pile than the committee of the traders' association had requested, because she couldn't bear the thought of a child turning up and not being able to have a book. Meg from Tiny Tim's Toys was supplying some presents too, but it was traditional for Santa to give each of the children a book at Gift Day, and she couldn't let the side down. It was a good job Rosie had volunteered to help her out with the wrapping, as there were well over a hundred books to package up.

'Only me!' Rosie called up the stairs to the flat when she arrived, letting herself in with the spare key Maddie had given her in case of emergencies.

They'd become close almost instantly when Cecil's Adventures had opened, and it was great to have someone next door you could rely on. She had a key to Rosie's place, too: they looked out for each other, and it was like having family around.

'Come on up. I've got the kettle on and some chocolate brownies in the oven.' She smiled as the pace of Rosie's footsteps quickened. 'But you can't have any until you've wrapped at least ten books!'

'What if I told you I've got us some extra help?' Taking the oversized pink scarf from around her neck, Rosie draped it over the armchair next to her coat.

'It depends on who it is.' As she spoke, Maddie poured water into the Christmas teapot that had been her grandmother's. She'd had a whole tea service decorated with Christmas roses, which she'd only every brought out in December, and it was another tradition Maddie was upholding.

'I hope you don't mind, but I've invited Simon to come over.' Rosie made to grab a brownie, but Maddie was too quick for her — whipping the plate out of her way and laughing as her friend stuck out her bottom lip in response. 'Spoilsport!'

'Okay, you can have one straight away, seeing as you've invited Simon to join us.' She grinned. 'It will be great to see him again. I can sit him down and ask him what his intentions are.' She laughed again as Rosie shot her a look.

'You're worse than my mother! Ever since I mentioned the possibility of an engagement to her, she keeps asking when I'll be getting the ring.' Rosie gave one of her deep, throaty laughs. 'I knew I should have kept my mouth shut!'

'So when *are* we going to see a ring? Or have things changed?'

Rosie tapped her nose. 'All in good time, my friend, all in good time!'

'You do know that not one more crumb of brownie will pass your lips until you tell me, don't you?'

'I'll tell you when Simon gets here.' Rosie moved over to the iPod docking station. 'In the meantime, let's put on some music to really get us in the mood for Christmas.'

* * *

An hour later, they'd wrapped half of the books. Each of the rectangular packages was secured with a pretty bow. The committee would be charging the parents of the children attending Gift Day to see Santa Claus and receive a present. All the money raised would go to the children's hospital where David had once been a patient, to make sure the little ones there had the best Christmas possible too. It was a recent St Nicholas Bay tradition, but nonetheless very much a part of the build up to the big day.

'That'll be Simon!' Dropping the book she'd been wrapping as soon as they heard the knock, Rosie bolted down the stairs. Anyone would think she hadn't seen Simon for ages!

Maddie thought briefly of Ben. That probably wasn't a good idea, though, since he'd disappeared after David's fundraiser without even saying good-bye. Much to her relief, the committee had since let her know that they'd received an email confirming the matched funding for the quiz night. So that was something, at least.

'Maddie, it's great to see you again! You look really well.' Simon kissed her on the cheek, the cold still clinging to his skin.

'Is that code for saying I've put on weight?' She laughed as he shook his head so vigorously that his glasses slid down his nose.

'Not at all, just that life here obviously suits you.'

'It does. In fact, I can barely remember a life before.' Maddie flicked the kettle on and set another cup and saucer on the tray. 'How about you? How's school?'

'Well, put it this way: I'm at a stage

where I can definitely imagine a life *after* the school. Sometimes it's the only thing that keeps me going! And, since meeting this wonderful woman — ' He turned to look at Rosie. ' — I've been re-evaluating my whole life.'

'We both have. In fact, you might want to sit down when you've made the tea.' Rosie looked almost nervous. 'We've got some big news.'

In the few moments it took for Maddie to finish making the tea and set out the rest of the brownies on one of her grandmother's flowered plates, a hundred thoughts raced through her head. Maybe they were expecting a baby; or about to announce a date for the wedding; or perhaps Simon was even going to give up teaching and go into business with Rosie in Belle's Brides. Although she couldn't really see him feeling comfortable giving advice to brides-to-be.

'Go on, then. I'm not sure I can take the suspense any longer!' Maddie put the tray on the coffee table opposite where Simon and Rosie were sitting hand in hand.

'I've been offered a job in Kentucky. I actually did my degree in Geography and Agriculture, but haven't really used the farming side of things since I graduated, although I've always wanted to. After a particularly bad week at school, I was searching online, wondering if there was more to life than teaching, when I saw an advert. I didn't really think I stood a chance, but I applied for it anyway. It was for a job with the state governor's office, working on a two-year farming project to support sustainability.' To Maddie, Simon was speaking Double Dutch, but she nodded politely.

'Like I said, I never dreamt I'd get the job — but they've even thrown in a relocation package, and it seems like the opportunity of a lifetime. For a start, there won't be an Ofsted inspector in sight!' He laughed at his own joke, and Maddie was torn between wanting to hug him and wanting to slap him. It was a brilliant opportunity for him; but, judging by the way Rosie was clinging to his hand, it almost certainly meant that everything was about to change for her too.

'When will you leave?' She forced a smile. He was setting off on an adventure and taking Rosie with him, but wasn't that the one thing her grandfather had always advocated? Just because setting up a shop in St Nicholas Bay made Maddie feel completely fulfilled, it didn't mean she should expect it to be the same for her friends.

'He's got to give the school three months' notice.' Rosie caught her eye, as if willing Maddie to be happy for them. 'So we're planning to leave at Easter, which should give me a chance to sell on the lease for the shop.'

Even though Maddie had been fully expecting it, when Rosie said the words out loud, it was as though someone had pushed her down into her seat with considerable force. Things just wouldn't be the same without Rosie next door.

'You're selling?' She bit her lip, determined not to ruin their big announcement with her own selfishness. 'I thought maybe you'd just sub-let while you were away.'

'I think most tenants will want a longer lease than that, and the Bay isn't the best place for a bridal shop in any case. The business rates here are only really worth paying if you've got a shop that's linked to the traditions of the Bay in some way, and most of my brides come from the neighbouring towns. So, if I do decide to set up again when we get home, I'd be better off opening somewhere else.' Rosie spoke more softly than usual, but even Maddie had to admit what she was saying made sense.

'It sounds like you've really thought it through.' She poured the tea robotically, wondering if she should offer to get some champagne, even though there was a big part of her that didn't feel like celebrating at all. 'So, are you still planning on having a wedding before you go?'

'No, we're going to wait for a bit, and there's absolutely no way I'll be having one at all without you there.' Rosie laughed so deeply that her head shook. 'And my mum will commit murder if she doesn't get her big mother-of-the-bride moment. As she's so fond of reminding me, she's waited long enough!'

'Have you thought about who you might sell to?' Maddie asked, trying not to think about Ben again, but it seemed Rosie could read her mind.

'Ben mentioned his firm are always looking out for commercial premises. I didn't take much notice at the time, but he left his business card with me, and I rang him yesterday. He's coming to talk to me about it, but I'm still not even sure what his firm does.' Rosie lifted another brownie on to her plate.

'It's something to do with catering, I think. I just hope it's not a butcher's or something like that. The smell of raw

meat won't mix well with my teashop.'
Maddie shuddered at the thought.

'Maybe it'll be a kebab shop instead?
You get some wonderful aromas from
those!' Rosie's deep laughed filled the
room again.

'As long as it's not a bakery or
another tearoom, I should be okay.'
Another wave of panic swept through
her, but she forced herself to push it
down. Surely Ben would have mentioned something like that?

She wasn't going to worry about it
for now. It might come to nothing,
anyway, and she just wanted to enjoy
the evening with Rosie. After all, she
didn't know how many more of those
she had left.

The rest of the night passed in easy
conversation. In between lots of
laughter, a whole plate of chocolate
brownies, and the opening of some
sparkling wine in lieu of champagne,
they somehow managed to wrap the
rest of the books. Despite her misgiv-
ings and her own feelings about Rosie

leaving, it was obvious to Maddie how well-suited she and Simon were, and how much in love. In the end, even she got caught up in their excitement. It was only when she packed the books into boxes after they'd left, and turned off the Christmas lights, that the flat suddenly felt lonely. Turning up Wham!'s 'Last Christmas' on her iPod to drown out the silence, she picked up a leftover copy of *The Gruffalo's Child*, slowly turning the pages. If that didn't cheer her up, nothing would.

★　★　★

David was splashing in the waves, seemingly oblivious to the near-freezing temperature of the water. Although the meningitis had left him with a moderate degree of cerebral palsy that restricted the natural movement of his hips, he didn't let that stand in his way. And he could be amazingly fast on his feet when he put his mind to it. Maddie had the afternoon off, and couldn't think of a better way to spend it than on the beach with her favourite boy. Enid and the twins were running the shop and Becky was busy wrapping some of David's presents, so the two of them had gone for a mini-adventure on the beach. He was wrapped up in about six layers and they'd made a substitute 'snowman' out of sand on Main Beach, complete with a carrot nose and some driftwood for arms. Now he was splashing through the white foam as the waves turned over on the sand at Half Moon Cove, and shrieking with excitement every time a new surge rolled in.

Half Moon Cove was a tiny bay at the far end of the promenade, which hardly anyone found even in the height of summer. You had to be a local to know it was there, and almost everyone stuck to the much sandier Main Beach by the harbour that led up to the shops and restaurants.

A huge bank of rocks separated Half Moon Cove from Main Beach, and the only way to reach it, unless the tide was right out, was down a flight of stone steps. The stone had been worn away over years of high tides, so that the edges were uneven and potentially lethal, especially when receding waves left seaweed as their parting gift. It was Maddie's favourite place, and somewhere she and David could come without the danger of a big dog bounding over to him at any point. It wasn't that he didn't love animals, but his hearing problems meant that he didn't always hear people — or other noises — when they weren't directly in front of him, and Becky had told her that he'd been knocked flying by a dog more than once in the past. The receding tide had shifted to leave a ten-foot strip of sand between banks of pebbles. Maddie smiled; she'd be able to write to her grandfather today.

With David happily paddling on the edge of the waves, she turned to check they were still alone, and moved towards the patch of sand. It was smooth and unblemished, not even a strand of seaweed spoiling the writing surface. There was a perfect stick on the pebbles behind it, too. It had been shaped by its journey, by the waves it had travelled on, and was now gnarled and knobbly like the finger of a skeleton, but with a perfect point at one end.

She wrote to her grandfather, just as she had done since the first days after he'd died. His ashes had been scattered in the sea, so there was no urn to chat to, no gravestone where she could pour out her heart. Instead, writing to him on the sand had become a habit over the past five years. She always told him that she loved him and missed him, what she'd been up to — her latest 'adventures', as he would have called them — about the great books she'd read, and sometimes she'd even ask him a question. He never answered, of course, not directly, but the answer always came to her just the same. Perhaps it was the act of writing it down that helped, although anyone watching would have thought she was crazy.

* * *

Ben's head was still spinning with the events of the past few days, and the night of the fundraiser in particular. It had been a long time since he'd questioned what he was doing with his life in that way. He needed some air; he couldn't make contact with Rosie about selling the lease until he'd made some kind of sense of what it was he was feeling.

There were at least two hours of daylight left, but the light was already beginning to change. He hadn't sat on a beach for years, yet the sounds were still familiar from those days spent fishing with his dad. It had been their thing to do together — without his mum and little brother — quality time that he hadn't dreamt would be so short-lived. He'd found the steps down to Half Moon Cove quite by accident, but the emptiness of the beach had appealed to him, so he'd made his way over the rocks that hid it so effectively.

Ridiculously dressed for clambering across stone, his leather-soled shoes slipped on the mossy seaweed, and his coat weighed too heavily for him to move as freely as he wanted to. Still he climbed on, until he reached the very centre of the bank of rocks, almost out of sight of everything but the sea itself, the beaches just visible in the distance. He sat there for a long while, the cold grey sea stretching ahead, searching for an answer to the dilemma that had been playing on his mind since the quiz. At first, it had been bitterly cold, but after a while he stopped feeling it — almost as if he'd gone numb to that, too.

He wasn't sure how long he'd been there — maybe an hour — when he looked up and realised that Maddie had arrived on the beach. She was looking furtively around her as though she were about to bury a body, whilst the little boy she was with played on the edge of the water. Of course, there was no body. She just wrote in the sand: lines and lines, looking up all the time to make sure her charge was still safe. He couldn't make out what it was she was writing; but one thing was certain, she hadn't seen him.

★ ★ ★

Maddie had finished her message by the time she noticed Ben, dressed as though he were headed for some stuffy business meeting, scrambling down the rocks in much the same way as a child might have done.

Going hot at the thought of him watching what she'd been doing, she dropped the stick on the floor and hastily scuffed the sand over with her feet. Usually she liked the idea of the sea taking her words with it, as if they somehow had a better chance of finding her grandfather that way, ridiculous as that was. This time, she had no choice but to erase the words: the prospect of letting Ben see them made her insides curl over.

'Are you okay?' The words were out of her mouth before she could stop them. He looked frozen stiff. Despite how angry she'd felt at him for rushing off from the fundraiser without a word, she still liked him. Try as she might to deny it, the attraction was there — whether she wanted it to be or not. This was the last place she'd expected to see him, though — he looked so out of place on the beach.

'Actually, I was about to ask you the same thing.' Ben looked down at the scuffs in the sand that she'd just made with her feet.

'What, this?' She hesitated. There was something about his expression that hinted he might understand. But even Rosie didn't know about the letters in the sand. It was her secret, not something to share with someone she barely knew. Before she could answer, David came towards them, putting his gloved hand in hers and regarding Ben with a somewhat suspicious look.

'David, this is Ben. He bought *The Gruffalo* for his niece on your recommendation.' She squeezed his hand to reassure him, and the little boy smiled at the mention of his favourite story.

'It's a good book.' David gave Ben a thumbs-up sign with his other hand, and then released his grip on Maddie, instantly distracted by the hunt for the perfect shell — which had been his mission, on and off, for as long as Maddie could remember.

'I brought him down so Becky could get some of his Christmas presents wrapped up. I was trying to work out a design for the poster to advertise a book launch we're having, whilst he was playing in the water. It's for a novel called *Writing In The Sand*.' Quite where the lie had come from, and so quickly, was a complete mystery to Maddie.

'Sounds interesting. What's it about?' He was smiling, as if he could see right through what she'd said, but she wasn't about to give him the satisfaction of confessing. After all, he still hadn't apologised for disappearing from the fundraiser. And admitting you wrote letters in the sand to your dead grandfather wasn't an easy thing to do.

'It's got an unusual plot.' She smiled, trying not to panic. This was exactly why she didn't like lying; it always seemed to spiral out of control. Now she had to make up a plot of a book that didn't even exist. 'It's a thriller, about a boat captain who murders his passengers, but the author's keeping the full story pretty close to his chest. He's cagey like that.'

'Seems like the sort of book I might enjoy. Who's it by?' Ben gave her a quizzical look.

'His name's, er . . . ' Maddie searched around, desperate for inspiration. ' . . . Flint Sandstone.'

'Is he local? It sounds like an American name.'

'You're right. He's from the States originally, I think, but he settled near the Bay a while back.' She was getting hot again, and desperate to change the subject. 'So what about you? Why were you climbing over a load of slimy rocks in your Sunday best?'

'I was looking for something.' The amused look he'd been wearing slid off his face.

'Really? Anything I can help with?'

'Not unless you know where to find the answer to an impossible question.' There was a weariness about him, and she wanted to reach out. But, given that he'd run off into the night just after they'd shared their first kiss, maybe that wasn't such a good idea.

'A moral dilemma?'

'Something like that.' He didn't elaborate, and she didn't push. Instead, she found a smooth, flat pebble and handed it to him.

'Try this. My granddad always said that if you skim stones for long enough, the answer will come to you eventually.'

'O-kay.' He said the word slowly, giving her another of the quizzical looks he did so well. 'And is there some logic to this theory?'

'Apparently, it's something to do with having to concentrate, so that your mind goes blank of all other thoughts and lets the answer in.' She picked up a few more pebbles which were the perfect size and shape. 'Only I'll warn you, I'm not very good at it. I've been trying to teach David for ages, but even he gave up on me in the end!'

At the mention of his name, the little boy abandoned his search for shells and stood next to Maddie. The three of them must have spent half an hour throwing pebbles towards the sea; and Ben, perhaps predictably, was an expert. All Maddie's attempts plopped into the water with a loud splash, which had him shaking with laughter at one point. Especially when David now picked up the technique with considerable ease. She tried one approach that almost wiped the smile permanently off Ben's face — for the only skimming was that of the stone as it flew past his cheek!

'Do you want me to show you?' He gave her such an appraising look, it was all she could do to nod. Moving behind her, he placed his arm along hers, showing her how to move so the pebble could skim rather than sink straight into the grey depths. It took several attempts, but eventually it worked. Caught up in the euphoria as her pebble finally bounced across the surface of the water, she turned, wrapping her arms around his neck.

'I can't believe I've done it — I mean, *we've* done it!' She laughed and he swung her around in a circle, both of them caught up in the simple joy of the moment. When he put her down, there was the briefest of pauses, as though he was going to kiss her again . . . until a seagull screaming at its flock broke the tension.

'Congratulations, Maddie, you're almost as good as this young man.' Ben looked towards David, who smiled in response. He'd stockpiled a small mountain of pebbles next to him, throwing one after the other into the water. It seemed that the search for the perfect shell was over — a new pastime in its place.

'I couldn't have done it without you.' She meant every word, and it had been so much fun; but the near-miss of another kiss made her feel awkward in his presence again. He hadn't even mentioned the night of the fundraiser, but it was like a cloud hanging over them.

'Look, I've been wanting to say something about the other night, but I didn't want to make things worse.' Ben placed a hand on her arm, almost as if he'd been reading her thoughts — that seemed to be happening to her a lot lately.

'Worse than what? I thought we were getting along, I thought we were . . . ' She stopped. This was getting really embarrassing now.

'We were, and it's not you, it's . . . ' She waited for him to add the word 'me' — that old line, the most clichéd of all brush-offs when you were trying to spare someone's feeling. But he didn't say it. 'It's this place, I guess. It's made me question a few things, and the way you all pulled together at the fundraiser made me realise I haven't had that for a long time. Roots, I mean; somewhere I could actually call home. It's stupid, but I was feeling a bit sorry for myself, and maybe even panicking a bit about what I might be getting into with renting Sarah-Jane's house.' He bent down, skimming another stone perfectly across the water.

'But if it's something you envied, then wouldn't moving to the Bay be the best thing you could do?' Maddie kept her voice level, determined not to let him know just how much she hoped he would take the lease of the cottage. He clearly wasn't someone who liked feeling cornered.

'Maybe, but my work involves being on the move all the time, and two years is a long commitment.'

'Have you ever thought about changing your job, so you can make a proper home in one place?' Maddie didn't miss the way his face clouded over at her words — it was almost as if the sun had hidden itself for a moment, deepening the shadows on his face.

'Sometimes, but I chose my career for lots of reasons, and if there have been sacrifices along the way, then I have to say they've been worth it.' He took her hand for a moment. 'But it's been a long time since I've met someone like you; and, if you can forgive me for the way I acted after the fundraiser, then I promise I won't just do a disappearing act again.'

'It doesn't count unless you pinkie-promise.' David looked up from where he'd been adding to his pile of stones. Even with his hearing impairment, when he was standing close enough, he didn't miss a trick.

'He's right, you know.' Ben smiled, letting go of her hand, and crooked his little finger, holding it out towards her.

'Okay, I pinkie-promise that I won't disappear if you agree to come out with me again, and I promise to make it up to you. We can have the date anywhere you choose, doing whatever you like best.'

Maddie had hooked her finger around his and was debating exactly where it was she'd ask him to take her — maybe to the new Mexican that had just opened, Nachos on the Bay — when her phone rang, and she quickly withdrew her hand.

Taking the mobile out of her pocket, she saw that the call was from Rosie; giving Ben an apologetic look, she answered.

'Oh, thank goodness!' Rosie sounded breathless. 'I was worried you weren't going to pick up, and I've run out of ideas!'

'What's up?' Given Rosie's tendency to overdramatise the situation, Maddie wasn't too worried. She smiled as Ben leant down to help David find yet more stones for his skimming pile. He'd done very well at redeeming himself this afternoon, and she wouldn't even hold him to letting her choose where their next date was; not if there was somewhere else he'd rather go.

'You know Kate's dad is always Santa Claus for the Gift Day, and the Henderson twins were going to be his two elves?' Rosie's speech was getting faster and faster. Whatever it was she had to say, it really shouldn't warrant this level of panic.

'Yes, what's the matter? Kate's dad isn't ill, is he?' That was the only thing she could think of which could be causing Rosie so much concern.

'No, but one of the girls has won tickets on some radio show to a concert in London that's got all their favourite bands. They've been in tears about missing the Gift Day and letting everyone down, but they're beside themselves because they so want to go. You weren't here to make the decision, so I told them they could, thinking someone else would be able to step into the breach, but it seems like everyone else is already busy doing something for Gift Day. I've managed to persuade Simon to dress up as an elf. But that routine they do with Santa when they're giving out the presents — you know, the one about the good elf and his naughty twin — means there absolutely has to be two of them. I can't think of anyone, and it needs to be a man if they're supposed to be Simon's twin, preferably someone about the same height.'

'What about Ben?' She grinned as she said his name. He'd made a promise — in front of David, of all people — although he'd had no way of knowing what he was getting himself into at the time.

'Ben?' Rosie's voice had risen by another octave. 'He'll never agree to that, surely?'

'Oh, I think he will.' She was laughing now, watching Ben enjoying himself with David, not knowing the fate that awaited him. 'Just leave it with me, and I'll call you back as soon as I can to confirm.'

'Everything okay?' Ben stood upright as Maddie walked back towards them. He still wasn't sure why it was so important for her to give him a second chance, but he was really glad she had. There was a whimsical smile on her face, like someone with a secret, and for some reason he desperately wanted to know what it was.

'You know that promise you just made me?' She raised an eyebrow and he nodded in response. Wherever it was she wanted to go on their date was fine by him. 'Well, I think I'm about to call it in. And you did say anything and anywhere, didn't you?'

'He pinkie-promised.' David said the words very seriously, just in case there was a chance that Ben might have forgotten.

'I did.' Ben caught Maddie shooting David a subtle wink — not subtle enough for him to miss it though. Suddenly, he wasn't sure he wanted to hear what she had to say after all.

'That's settled, then. We'll go to the Gift Day tomorrow.' She was still smiling, and it all sounded fairly pain-free so far.

'The Gift Day?' He thought he'd seen a poster advertising it at The Quill and Ink, but there were so many community events that he hadn't really taken it in.

'Yes, it's an annual event where parents bring their children to see Santa and the elves hand out some presents, and all the money raised goes to the hospital that treated David when he was poorly.' There was something about Maddie's expression that gave the game away. There was more to this than met the eye, that was for certain, and he didn't have to wait much longer to find out what.

'Presumably you've donated some books?' Ben asked, and she nodded. 'So what will we be doing on this date?'

'Well, I'm doing a reading from a couple of classic Christmas stories, and you'll be dressed as an elf!' She was grinning as she spoke, and he wasn't sure at first if he'd even heard her correctly.

'An elf?' He turned the words over, and it felt almost like he was speaking another language, the concept was so alien.

'Yes, with green tights and everything. Rosie's boyfriend Simon has volunteered too.' She paused and inclined her head towards David, widening her eyes. 'Because Santa needs some extra-special help, and the girls who were taking part have had to drop out.'

'Volunteered? Is that what I've done?' He couldn't help smiling; he'd fallen right into this trap. It was a darn good job he was a bit more cautious when it came to making promises in his business negotiations.

'Well, you did pinkie-promise.' Maddie looked towards David, who nodded sagely in agreement.

'In that case — and I can't quite

believe I'm saying this — consider me in.' Ben shook his head. The thought of parading around in green tights was hardly appealing, but he didn't want to let Maddie down again, and working alongside Rosie's boyfriend for the day might not be a bad strategy for finalising the deal on Belle's Brides.

'I'm looking forward to it already!' Maddie finally gave in to the laughter she'd clearly been struggling to hold back, linking her left arm through his and taking David's hand in her right. 'First stop is Rosie's for a costume fitting.'

They headed up the beach, with Ben still trying to work out how he'd been so expertly roped into taking part in the Gift Day. St Nicholas Bay was certainly full of surprises.

7

The morning of Gift Day dawned bright and crisp. Wispy white clouds drifted across a bright blue sky and, other than the chill in the air, it could have been a spring day rather than just a week before Christmas.

For once, Maddie had closed up the shop early, so that she could make the most of the afternoon. The children from St Nicholas Bay Primary School were performing at the opening, before Santa and his elves took to the stage — she couldn't help laughing every time she thought of Ben in those promised green tights. He'd texted her to say he was spending the morning with Simon and Kate's dad, rehearsing, and that she owed him a date of his choice when it was all over. At least he wanted to see her again, despite her volunteering him as an elf, so maybe they'd get that meal at Nachos on the Bay after all. David was singing with the school choir, and she wouldn't miss that for the world either.

Everyone would be down by the harbour today anyway — even the tourists would head down there on Gift Day, rather than up the high street to the shop — so there was no real point in staying open and missing out on anything.

'Look at this!' Rosie was already waiting outside when Maddie locked up the shop, ready to head down the hill in time for the start of the singing. She held up her mobile phone, her throaty laugh making other people turn to look at them. 'Simon sent me a picture of him and Ben in all their finery. It's even funnier than I thought.'

Maddie took the phone, and had to press her lips together to stop herself laughing even louder than her friend. Ben was wearing exactly the sort of green tights she'd imagined, a droopy hat with a bell on the end that Noddy would have been proud of, a candy-cane-striped waistcoat, oversized ears, and a pained expression that said more than words ever could.

'Oh wow, that's pretty awful, isn't it?' She couldn't stop the laughter any longer: it bubbled up, setting Rosie off again, who was now laughing so much she had to wipe her eyes with the back of her hand.

They'd just about regained their composure by the time they reached the harbour. A huge Christmas tree stood at the side of the area where the primary school choir was already starting to gather. The tree looked rather bare, but there were strings of unlit lights half-hidden in the foliage. By the time the day was over, it would be hung with stars, and a thousand tiny lights would be turned on to commemorate lost loved ones from the town. It was another St Nicholas Bay tradition, originally started to honour local sailors lost at sea, but now open to anyone who wanted to remember a loved one at Christmas.

Lots of the boats were decorated with fairy lights too, but they didn't look nearly so impressive in the daylight. Maddie watched Kate trying to organise her class into neat rows; but, the children being so young, it was a bit like trying to herd cats, and it wasn't until some of the mothers got involved that they managed to get the group into something resembling a choir.

David waved as he caught sight of Maddie, and she gave him a quick thumbs-up sign. It was a classic repertoire of children's Christmas carols — everything from 'Little Donkey' through to 'Away in a Manager', and even a French version of 'Silent Night'. The small chapel, situated on the edge of the harbour, which was dedicated to the patron saint of sailors — St Nicholas — was too small to accommodate all of the Gift Day activities. So they took place mostly out in the open, with only a canvas canopy over the stage to protect them from the elements. Luckily, this year it was promising to stay dry.

'It makes you want to have one of your own, doesn't it?' Rosie whispered as the children started their final song.

'I think I'm a long way off that yet, but it could be you sometime soon.' Maddie was slowly coming to terms with the prospect of her friend being halfway around the world for the next two years. She only hoped she'd come home if she did decide to start a family. Maddie was determined to be the best aunt and godmother she could to her friend's children. Not having brothers or sisters of her own, she was more than happy to take on that mantle — David already called her Auntie Mads. She was trying not to think much beyond the next few days, anyway, let alone the next few years. After their afternoon on the beach, it was no good pretending that her attraction to Ben was casual. But, unless he took the cottage on, he'd be gone in a few days.

'You never know.' Rosie squeezed her arm. Despite getting rid of most of her soppy novels, she was still a die-hard romantic at heart. 'Ben rang me last night to say he wanted to talk a bit more about buying the lease to Belle's tomorrow morning. He's hoping to tie up the deal at the same time as the lease for Sarah-Jane's place.'

'Really? He's going through with the cottage?' Maddie's voice came out much louder all of a sudden, and one or two of the crowd turned to look at her.

'That's what he said, but we'll talk about it later.' Rosie laughed, attracting much more attention than Maddie had. 'After all, we don't want to get banned from the audience before we've had a chance to see the boys in those green tights.'

★ ★ ★

'You were brilliant!' Maddie pulled David into a hug, and he flung his arms around her neck. Rosie had headed off to help dress the girls from Kate's class who were playing the angels in the next part of the show, having supplied the costumes every year since she'd opened her shop.

'I remembered all the words, Auntie Mads! Do you think Santa could see me? Maybe he'll bring the castle if he saw what a good boy I've been.'

Becky stood behind him and winked at her friend. The castle was due in any day now, and Maddie had bought some wooden soldiers to go with Becky's present for her son. The two of them were almost as excited at the prospect as David was — but not quite.

'I'm sure he was watching and you'll definitely be on the good list after that. What about your lines for the nativity on Tuesday, do you know them all off by heart?' Maddie pulled the woolly hat, that was threatening to rise up off his head, down a bit — being careful not to cover his hearing aid.

'I know *all* my lines.' David beamed with pride.

'And everybody else's, I should think!' Becky laughed. 'Kate's been brilliant with them, and there's a trainee teacher, Jack, who's been working one-to-one with him too. It's made a world of difference to his reading.'

'You won't need me to come and read to you for much longer, then?' Maddie's insides twisted at the thought. Babysitting David was a joy, and the fact he'd eventually grow out of her storytelling wasn't something she'd considered before.

'I like being read to best, even though I'm getting good. Jack does stories too, but he doesn't do the voices like you, 'cos he's old.' David gave a matter-of-fact shrug, and Maddie looked questioningly at his mum.

'What David means is that Jack is old compared to the other trainee teachers they've had in the class. I spoke to him at the parents' evening last week, and he told me he'd decided to retrain as a teacher when he turned forty. You know what it's like when you're a kid; forty seems positively ancient.' There was something in the tone of Becky's voice which suggested more than a passing interest in this trainee teacher, and Maddie found herself smiling at the prospect of her friend starting to date again. Her own love life might have been stalled for a long time, and it was very early days with Ben, but since Rosie's news it suddenly seemed like love was in the air all over St Nicholas Bay.

'And what else did this Jack say?' She was teasing now, but the colour on Becky's cheeks suggested she'd been spot on.

'Nothing! He's nice, okay? Stop giving me a hard time!' She was laughing, though, and it was the nicest sound in the world. The previous two Gift Days, since Henry had died, had been incredibly difficult. That first year, when Becky had been invited by the vicar to be the first to hang a star on the memorial tree, she'd needed physical support to make it to the harbour-side, and the prospect of her laughing on the day of the annual ceremony would have seemed impossible to Maddie. If there was anyone who deserved to be happy, it was Becky. Maddie still had every intention of speaking to Kate about Jack later, though, to make sure he was everything he seemed to be. Anyone who broke Becky's heart would have the whole of the Bay to answer to.

'I've got something for you, actually — they came in today.' Becky handed her a brown paper bag as David wriggled out of her arms and went to join his friends at the front of the stage, where Santa was about to make his grand entrance. 'I hope you like them.'

Maddie carefully lifted a small wooden Christmas ornament out of the bag. It was an almost perfect replica of the wooden plane and its pilot that was suspended from the ceiling in Cecil's Adventures — the one that Ben had hit his head on the night they'd kissed. Peering into the bag, she could see another one, exactly the same.

'Oh, Becky, they're perfect! Where on earth did you find them?' Looking up at her friend, she had to press her lips together again, this time to stop herself crying.

'It's all down to the power of the internet.' Becky squeezed her hand. 'I thought you could put one on the memorial tree and one on your tree at home to remember Cecil. I still think of him every time I pass the old library building.'

'It's so incredible of you to think about me when the ceremony is so much more poignant for you.'

'Just because Henry was younger and he died more recently, it doesn't give me the right to think my grief is more important than anyone else's.' Becky pulled a wooden figure of a father cradling his son out of her pocket. 'David and I are going to hang this on the tree for Henry too, but I really wanted you to have something special for your grandfather. He'd be so proud of you, you know, and anyone walking into your shop can tell how much he meant to you. Anyway, given that you lost him at Christmas, this is just as important to you as it is to me.'

'We're really going to need Ben and Simon to turn up in those green tights soon to lighten the mood.' Maddie tried to laugh, the back of her throat burning with a whole range of other emotions. 'What with David singing in the choir, and thinking about Granddad and how proud Henry would be to see how you're raising your son, I'm not sure how much more I can take!'

As it turned out, they didn't have long to wait. Less than five minutes later, the new head of the traders' association, Paul Turner, who ran Marley's Chains, the DIY store, took to the stage.

'Ladies and gentleman, boys and girls, the moment you've all been waiting for. Please welcome Santa and his elves — Dippy and Chippy — to the stage!'

'Dippy and Chippy! I wonder which

is which?' Rosie, who had finished dressing the angels, was standing between Maddie and Becky, filming every moment of Simon and Ben's stint as elves on her mobile phone.

'I don't know, but they're doing a really good job of pretending they're enjoying themselves.' Maddie didn't even try to stop the laughter this time; and, if the expression on Ben's face was anything to go by, she didn't need to. He actually looked like he was having fun and he was a natural at engaging the crowd of young children at the front of the audience, getting them to call out lines like they were part of a pantomime. Maybe he'd inherited some of his mum's skills — he'd mentioned she was a drama teacher — but, whatever it was, he seemed to have found a new vocation.

★ ★ ★

Becky had taken David to see the real reindeer that the traders' association had hired for the day, and Rosie had gone with Simon to find a coffee, since he was in desperate need of a warm-up after standing around in tights for the last half an hour. Maddie was waiting for Ben as soon as he came off the stage.

'Do you know what, I'd never have believed that performance if I hadn't seen it with my own eyes!'

'And I'd never have believed I'd enjoy it!' He laughed and reached up to remove his ears.

'Don't!' Placing her hand over his, she stopped him. 'The kids will see, and you'll spoil the magic.'

'Of course, sorry.' He looked into her eyes for what seemed like an eternity, her hand still over his. Moving towards her, he kissed her lightly on the lips . . . and this time there was no wooden plane to clonk him on the head! Although, given that they were surrounded by crowds of people, it was all very innocent: just the sort of kiss you might expect one of Santa's elves to give his girlfriend. Was that what she was, his girlfriend? All this dating stuff was made even more complicated by the fact that no-one actually seemed to come out and say these things.

'What was that for?' It was the closest she was going to come to asking him where this was all going. She couldn't help replaying the conversation with Rosie in her head — he was planning to stay in the Bay. That had to mean something, didn't it? Maybe this was why she'd stuck to concentrating on the business for so long: the rules were so much simpler.

'Call it a festive kiss. It's suddenly starting to feel a lot like Christmas.' He gave her a slow smile which lit up his brown eyes, changing the look of his whole face with it. 'Well, that and the fact I've been wanting to kiss you again ever since the night of the fundraiser.'

'Well, thank you, Mr Elf, it's the nicest Christmas kiss I've had *today*.' She laughed at the expression on his face.

'In that case, I need to up my game, don't I? How about dinner tomorrow night?'

'That sounds great. I've been wanting to try out that new Mexican — Nachos on the Bay. And, if you haven't already seen it, the harbour looks great at night this time of year; all the boats decorated with lights.' The memorial tree would be lit up by then, too, with Cecil's wooden plane hanging from one of the branches.

'You know, I thought I'd find all this Christmas overload stuff in St Nicholas Bay a bit too much, but it's having an unexpected effect on me. I haven't felt this Christmassy in years.' His ears moved half an inch upwards as he smiled.

'Just wait until after they decorate the tree and I've read the children's Christmas stories. If you don't feel like baking your own gingerbread house after that, then you really are the Grinch.'

'As long as it doesn't involve any

more dressing up. I might just get changed before they start decorating the tree. Otherwise, I could get too used to the tights — they're surprisingly comfortable!' Ben kissed her again, briefly, and turned to weave his way through the crowd, which took a lot longer than he might have expected as all the children wanted to talk to him. Maddie put her hand in the paper bag, running her fingers over one of the ornaments nestled there, the wood smooth under her touch. Was it a sign from Cecil? Just before Ben had appeared on the beach, she'd been writing to him, asking if the balance of her existence had somehow become skewed, and if it was time to take Rosie's advice and try out 'real' life. Now it seemed that another adventure was about to start, but it wasn't one where she could read the ending in advance. It was scary, but it felt right so far. That was the thing with real life — you never quite knew how it was going to turn out.

★ ★ ★

Ben returned to the edge of the stage just as Maddie took her seat at the centre of a semicircle of children, sitting cross legged and waiting for the story to begin. She read the classics — *The Night Before Christmas*; *The Snowman*; and, of course, a version of *A Christmas Carol*, which had been adapted and shortened for a younger audience. Ben's mother would have loved Maddie. She had a way of reading the stories that caught your attention, and the children who were sat at her feet were enraptured; but the adults in the crowd were quiet too, all looking in her direction. She acted out the parts in the stories, using a range of different voices, and never once getting mixed up. The children giggled in all the right places, and joined in with some of the classic lines that they obviously knew so well. It wasn't just St Nicholas Bay that was changing his mind about Christmas.

* * *

'Do you know if you hadn't already sold me all those books, I'd be queuing outside your shop until it opened so I could buy them.' He held out one of the cardboard cups of mulled cider he'd bought from a stall on the side of the harbour. 'Have you ever thought about taking up acting? Mum would love to have you in her Am Dram group. It's a shame she lives miles away.'

'It is.' Maddie took the cup from him, warming her hands on the outside of it as she stamped her feet. 'Although I don't think I'd inflict my acting on anyone. I had to keep up that performance just to stop myself freezing to death on that stage!'

'Don't sell yourself short. You were wonderful, your passion for the stories comes through so strongly.'

'I just retell them the way my grandfather used to. He ran the library in the Bay before the council closed it, and I used to spend hours there with him, listening to him read stories from his favourite books to me. It was better than watching a film, and I guess I just caught the storytelling bug.' She smiled and took a sip of the spicy cider. 'I do sometimes think about writing a children's book, but I've spent so much time getting the shop on its feet and running at a profit that I just haven't had time to get any further than thinking about it.'

'It's good to have a dream, I suppose, but I think you've got your priorities right. Making a living has to be the most important thing you do.' Ben had weighed the equation up more than once, and stability always won out over dreams.

'Luckily for me, the shop *is* my dream. If I do write something, it will just be part of that.' Maddie took another sip of her drink. 'What about you? Is there something else you'd like to do? I know when we talked about it before you said that circumstances had changed your plans.'

'I haven't really thought about it.' That wasn't true. Just lately, he'd been thinking about it a lot, and part of Ben wanted to tell her more about his father and what he'd grown up wanting to do. But what was the point? That particular dream had been long buried. 'All I've ever really wanted is to earn enough money so I don't have to worry about it. I trained as a surveyor, and then got into a project management that drew on those skills, which had exactly the sort of rewards I hoped it would.'

'And this firm of yours, what sort of catering do they do?' Maddie fixed him with a steady look and he wondered how much he should say. He'd been half-hoping lately that Rosie would decide not to sell, but he was due to meet her in the morning to discuss the terms, and she'd know then it was Hemmingway's he worked for. Now wasn't the right time to tell Maddie, though. It would be better over dinner, and they could talk more then about her plans to write — maybe she could even use the money from selling up Cecil's Adventures to fund the time. After all, there'd be no point her holding out on selling her lease if they bought Belle's Brides and opened up a coffee shop next door.

'I guess you'd call it a wine bar.' It certainly wasn't the whole truth, but it would have to do for now — until he found a way of framing it in a more positive light, and knew exactly how much Hemmingway's were willing to offer for Maddie's lease.

'Thank goodness! I was worried for a moment that it might be a sandwich bar or tearoom.' Maddie linked an arm through Ben's as they turned to face the stage again, where family members were beginning to line up to hang stars on the memorial tree, a message to their absent loved ones written on the back of each one. She turned to smile at him as David and Becky made their way across the stage, and a pang of what felt very much like guilt gripped his insides again.

8

Maddie had turned the shop upside down looking for it, and now she was doing the same with the flat. It had to be there somewhere. A wooden Christmas ornament couldn't just disappear into thin air. She'd hung the first one on the memorial tree, and had thought she'd put the other one in with her bag of books. Only, when she'd got home, it wasn't there. Racing back down to the harbour, she wondered if she'd dropped it somewhere en route, but there was no sign of it. Of course, someone could have picked it up, but she'd been so certain she'd put it in her bag. She could even visualise zipping the holdall shut. But she'd checked all the pockets in the bag and it wasn't there. She tried to stop looking, telling herself that if she had taken it out of the bag and put it in the flat or shop somewhere the night before, then it would turn up at some point, but she just couldn't seem to stop searching.

Looking at her watch as she closed a drawer she'd already opened ten times before, she realised with a jolt that it was only an hour until Ben was due to come and pick her up for their date. Putting her hand up to her hair, she could tell it looked a mess; hardly a surprise, given that she'd spent most of the day tearing through the shop and flat like a mad woman, looking for a little wooden plane.

She'd just stepped out of the shower, a towel wrapped around her head and a fluffy pink bathrobe doing the job of drying her — whilst she had one more quick look for the plane — when she heard the front doorbell ring.

'Oh, no — please tell me that's not Ben turning up early, tonight of all nights.' She said the words out loud to the empty flat; but, checking the clock over the fireplace, it couldn't be him. Not unless he was a full forty-five minutes early. She was just debating whether to answer the door or pretend to be out when someone called through the letterbox.

'Maddie, it's me. I didn't want to just let myself in because you weren't expecting me, but I've got something important to tell you.' Rosie sounded insistent: the last time she'd said something similar, she'd announced she was moving to the States. Maddie didn't have time for a long chat, and if she was going to go to her date dressed in something other than a bathrobe, she had to get a move on. Still, she wasn't in the habit of pretending to be out when it was one of her friends at the door, so she'd just have to tell Rosie to be quick.

'Come on up. It's okay, I'm decent.' Maddie glanced down at the old pink bathrobe again. 'Well, sort of.'

'Thank goodness you haven't gone out already.' Rosie — who sounded as if she'd bounded up the stairs two at a time — was breathless, her words coming out in gasps. 'Have you got anything to drink?'

'Of course, but Ben will be here in about forty minutes, so I can't be long. Do you want a coffee?' Maddie was already heading towards the kitchen.

'It's not for me, it's for you; but I think you might want something stronger.' Rosie's eyes darted towards Maddie. Whatever it was she had to say, it was obviously pretty significant.

'Okay, you're scaring me now. Let's skip the drinks and you can just tell me.' Maddie took a seat on one of the leather sofas, expecting Rosie to sit opposite her, but her friend was pacing like a cat on hot bricks.

'I met with Ben this morning about the lease, and he offered me three times more than I paid for it.'

'Wow, that's great. I suppose that means his company are really keen to get Belle's, then. I did tell him how hard it was to get commercial premises in the Bay.' Maddie rubbed her forehead, still not sure what all the fuss was about. 'Isn't that a good thing?'

'Well, it would be . . . if it wasn't a Hemmingway's they're planning to open.' Rosie finally sat down with a thud.

'It can't be — he told me it was a wine bar — ' Maddie felt as if she had been plunged underwater; nothing was making sense.

'They sell wine in the evenings now, but it's still the coffee shop that gets most of the trade; and now they're doing all those free downloads of books, too, and I know what you think of that idea!' Rosie was up on her feet again, an expression of pure indignation on her face. 'I didn't tell him straight away, because I wanted to talk to you first. But don't worry, I'm going to tell him he can stuff the offer where the sun doesn't shine. I don't care if he offers me a hundred times what I paid for it, there's no way I'd sell up to Hemming-way's.'

'But he's arranged to rent Sarah-Jane's place. Why would he do that if he was planning something like this? He'd hardly want to hang around, with the reaction that would provoke.'

'That's the other thing. I rang Sarah-Jane's husband after Ben left, I wanted to find out if Hemmingway's could just open up like that, and he said they had enough financial clout to do more or less what they want.' Rosie grimaced. 'And not only that, but he told me Ben had insisted on having a sub-let clause in his lease, even though they'd only agreed to do it if they could put the rent up by fifty percent. I'm sorry, Mads, but I don't think he was ever intending to hang around.'

'Right.' The towel slid down onto her shoulders as she spoke, her wet hair falling around her face. 'Thanks for telling me.' The words sounded hollow, even in her head.

'I'm so, so, sorry, but I couldn't not tell you.' Rosie moved next to Maddie, putting her arm around her shoulders. 'What are you going to do?'

'Well, I'm not going to be here when

he turns up, that's for sure.' She gave her best friend a brief hug and then stood up. 'So I'd better get some clothes on and get out of here. I can work out what on earth I'm going to do about Hemmingway's after that.'

★ ★ ★

The sky outside Ben's hotel room was inky black, a blanket of a thousand stars overlaying the darkness. Such a clear night meant they were almost certainly in for a heavy frost the next day. He wondered if St Nicholas Bay would deliver that most elusive of festive promises — at least in the South of England — and provide a white Christmas. There were still a few days to go, and he was due to leave on the twenty-third; but if Maddie did consider selling Cecil's Adventures, then there'd be enough reason to hang around. Rosie had seemed a bit shell-shocked when they'd met to discuss Hemmingway's offer, but the price had been very generous, and she wasn't the first person to have gone quiet until they got their head around it. With Belle's under his belt, he just hoped Maddie would see sense. It would be commercial suicide for her to try and keep the business going with a Hemmingway's next door. With the offer he was planning to make her, she'd probably have enough money to reopen Cecil's Adventures in a different location — another town nearby, maybe — and have some time off to write that book. She was business-minded, despite her sentiment, so she was bound to see sense in the end.

Putting his jacket on, he slipped his phone into the pocket, and headed down the stairs to the foyer of The Quill and Ink. The bar was visible from the reception: it was thronged with people, and someone was doing an appalling karaoke version of 'All I Want For Christmas'. An office party in full swing. He'd been planning on having a quiet drink, but it seemed preferable to give it a miss in the circumstances, so he found himself with twenty minutes to spare. Stepping outside into the relative peace of the hotel's car park, he took out his phone and scrolled down to Will's name in the contact list.

'Ben!' There was a hint of amusement in his brother's voice. 'It's not Christmas Day already, is it?'

'Alright, I know I've owed you a phone call for heaven knows how long, but better late than never, right?'

'It's always good to hear from you.' As Will spoke, Ben could make out the sound of a little girl singing in the background.

'How's Lily?' He hadn't seen his niece, or his brother, in over six months, and the little girl probably didn't have a clue who he was.

'She's brilliant, that's her singing. Her asthma's been playing up a bit, but nothing that slows her down.'

'And Jennie?' Ben began to walk as he talked. Conversations with his brother were never easy these days, and he didn't want to be late to meet Maddie.

'She's pregnant.' Will paused. 'Well, aren't you going to congratulate us?'

'I would, Will, but it hardly seems like the sensible thing for you to be doing, living in that flat and struggling on a research associate's income.' Ben gripped the phone. Maybe it wasn't such a bad thing; his brother might be more willing to take the cottage with another baby on the way, and not think of it as charity.

'It's only until I get my PhD, then I'll be earning much more. But we'll survive; we've got all we need.' Will sighed. 'And before you even ask, I'm not going to take any more of your handouts. You've been looking after me since we were kids, Ben, but I can stand on my own two feet now.'

'What about Lily? That flat you're living in's got damp, I told you that when you moved there. That can't be helping her asthma.' He kept his voice level, wanting to appeal to his brother's rational side, hoping it would override his pride. 'Surely you don't want to bring a new baby into that too?'

'What are you suggesting? That you buy a big house and we all move in with you?' Will's tone was dismissive. It was a running battle: Ben wanting to help — to show his love in the only way he really knew how — and Will wanting him to back off. But it was hard after so many years of playing the role his dad had left behind, of being the family provider. 'I'm not sure that would work, seeing as Lily doesn't know you from Adam.'

'I know I've been a rubbish uncle, but I've been staying in this little place on the coast — St Nicholas Bay — you could still get to the university in under an hour, and I've found the perfect cottage for you. Lily would love it here, they celebrate Christmas all year round, and there's the most fantastic toy shop that sells things like Dad used to make.'

'Blimey, Ben, you almost sound enthusiastic about something. Are you sure they haven't indoctrinated you into some sort of cult? What with the enthusiasm, and the unprecedented phone calls . . . ' Will might have been teasing, but there was a hint of bitterness in his voice.

'It's surprised me, I'll give you that. But you'll love it, and the cottage will be just up Jennie's street, the whole place is steeped in history.' His sister-in-law was an archaeologist, or at least she'd just finished her degree in archaeology when she'd married Will and fallen pregnant with Lily almost straight away.

'You're talking as if it's already a done deal.'

'Just come and look at it. And if you don't want to take it, I can always find someone else.' Ben sighed. Will's pride was getting in the way again, but if Jennie fell in love with the place, that might clinch the deal; and, if not, he could always sub-let it to someone else — that was the beauty of the clause he'd put in.

'I guess it's one way of guaranteeing we'll get to see you.' It was Will's turn to sigh. 'I don't suppose you've changed your mind about coming over for Christmas?'

'I just don't know what's happening yet. I've got to finalise a deal, and then there's Maddie . . . ' He hadn't meant to mention her, but somehow it had just slipped out.

'Maddie? Don't tell me there's a woman you want to get involved with down there, too. Whilst you're in the middle of a business deal?' Will sounded genuinely shocked. 'That's it, I'm coming down to find out who you are and what they've done with my real brother!'

'Oh, ha, ha, you're hilarious. She's just someone I've met whilst I've been scouting for properties, but she's — ' He hesitated. ' — nice.'

'Nice?'

'Well, okay, she's fun to be with.'

'Fun? Now I know they've been messing with your mind. Since when has Ben Cartwright been up for fun?'

'Well, it's given you a laugh.' He had to admit his brother was right, though. It had been a long time since he could remember experiencing as much fun as he had since he arrived in the Bay. If Will ever found out about his stint as an elf in those green tights, Ben would never hear the last of it. 'I've got to go, but I'll email you the details of that cottage and give you another call on Christmas Day.'

'Okay, I'll hold you to that call.' Will's voice was softer, the edge to his tone all gone. 'And, if you are managing to have fun, just carrying on doing whatever it is you've been doing down there.'

Ending the call, Ben smiled to himself as he walked the last hundred yards to Maddie's flat. If doing what he'd been doing meant seeing more of her, then he was definitely up for that. Only . . . after five minutes of knocking on her door and ringing the bell without an answer, he was beginning to realise she might not feel the same.

*　*　*

The lights strung on the masts of the boats didn't look nearly so festive through eyes that were blurred with tears. Maddie was upset — but, more than that, she was angry. Partly with herself, but mostly with Ben. True, she'd been foolish buying into the idea so readily peddled in Rosie's romance novels that a handsome stranger could just walk into your life out of the blue and change everything. But Ben was still the most to blame. He'd planned to change everything, all right — just not in the way she'd expected.

She hadn't even stopped to dry her hair; and, as much as she'd been desperate to leave the flat before he got there, that had been a mistake. Now she was cold as well as miserable, and walking around the edge of the harbour catching glimpses of everyone else having fun wasn't the best idea she'd ever had, either. She should have taken Rosie up on her offer and headed over to her flat, but she'd just wanted to be on her own. How long would she have to leave it before she headed home? She doubted Ben would be the sort to pine for hours on her doorstep; in fact, he probably didn't even care. What she couldn't work out was why he'd even wanted to take her out. Going after Rosie would have made more sense, if he'd had his eye on the lease to Belle's Brides all along. Unless he'd wanted Cecil's Adventures too . . .

That was it! It suddenly made sense, even if it didn't make her feel any better.

'Maddie!' She heard Ben's voice before she saw him. If she hadn't met his eyes, she'd have made a run for it. She didn't want to talk to him. There was nothing he could say that she didn't already know, and she'd only feel more of a fool if she had to hear it all over again from him.

'I'm not interested.' Quickening her pace, she headed past the memorial tree where, just the day before, everything had been so different.

'Maddie, stop! I want to know what's going on!' Ben was too quick for her and was by his side within seconds, his hand on her arm. 'What's wrong?'

'What's *wrong*?!' She was shouting, but she couldn't stop herself. 'How can you even stand there and ask me that when you work for Hemmingway's?' She almost spat the last word out, it tasted so bitter in her mouth.

'Rosie told you.' The calmness of his tone only made her angrier.

'Of course she did, she was horrified. But, trust me, her reaction wasn't a patch on mine!' Turning her back, she tried again to walk away from him, but he clearly wasn't giving up that easily.

'It's a good offer, and I can make an even better one to buy your lease, too. I'm not trying to drive you out of business. This could set you up — somewhere else, admittedly — but it would lift the financial pressure in a way that most people can only dream of.'

'Unlike you, I don't just dream about money!' If her words were cruel, then she was past caring. 'Cecil's Adventures is my dream, you know that; but Hemmingway's just wants to turn up and trample all over it. I'd rather die than sell you my lease, and Rosie feels the same.'

'You're not thinking about this logically.' His voice was still even, and she wanted to lash out at him, provoke a reaction, see if there was some genuine emotion behind his actions of the last few days. It was almost impossible to believe he was the same man who'd dressed up in green tights just to entertain some children. He certainly went the extra mile for this job of his.

'Think logically? Maybe not, but that's because I've got a passion for what I do. I don't suppose someone like you will ever understand that.' She shot him a look she hoped expressed the level of contempt she felt for him and his chain of coffee shops. 'So you might as well pack up those *generous* offers of yours and get out of the Bay for good, because no-one here is going to want to sell out to someone like you.'

'I wouldn't bank on it, Maddie. There are lots of businesses in St Nicholas Bay that aren't doing as well as yours, and lots of people who put stability over sentiment. It isn't a crime, you know.' There was finally a hint of emotion in those last few words. 'Maybe I should have been honest with you at the outset, but I wanted to try and make you see the benefits first, before you clouded it all with your preconceptions.'

'Well, doesn't that make you a saint?' She couldn't bear to hear another word. 'Just leave me alone. If I never see you again, it will be too soon.'

'Why are you being like this? Alright, so you don't want to sell your lease, but we can still go out. I like you, and I thought you felt the same.' He sounded confused, and for a moment she almost felt sorry for him — sorry he was so wrapped up in his job that he really couldn't see why she was so upset.

'I thought I liked you too. Only I didn't even know who you were back then.' Maddie pulled her coat more tightly around her body; the cold seemed to be seeping into her bones. 'And now that I do, I'm completely certain that you aren't worth a second more of my time.' Not stopping to hear his response, she started to run — worried for a moment that she could hear his footsteps behind her. But he hadn't followed her; and that, at least, was something to be thankful for.

★ ★ ★

By the time Ben got half-way back up the high street towards The Quill and Ink, he'd had a vitriolic text from Rosie telling him that she'd rather burn Belle's Brides down than sell it to him. The women of St Nicholas Bay certainly had strong opinions. Maybe he should have anticipated her reaction

— and the fact that Maddie would be the first person she told when she heard about Hemmingway's — but he could never have guessed exactly how fiercely they'd react. Yet he'd seen the other side of the Bay, and how the traders' association worked for the community. Business was only a small part of their lives. It was alien to him, and that was why he'd so badly misjudged the negotiations — but he wouldn't get caught out again. Martha's Tavernita, where he'd shared that first meal with Maddie, was running at a loss according to his research, and it had always been the back-up plan. He'd put in a call to the owner, Sebastian, in the morning. Trying not to think about the way Maddie had looked at him, he headed back up the stairs to his room. He'd get the deal done on the Tavernita as soon as possible, and put the rest behind him. The Bay was just one more location, after all, and his next job couldn't come too soon.

9

'Your call was a bit unexpected.' Sebastian ushered Ben through the door of Martha's Tavernita, glancing furtively to the left and right as if he was doing some sort of undercover criminal deal.

'I was originally negotiating for a different lease.' The smell of garlic and onions lingering from the night before made Ben's stomach lurch.

'I know, it's all over the Bay.' Sebastian gestured for him to take a seat at one of the wooden tables in the restaurant, and put a pot of coffee between them. 'Rosie rang everyone in the traders' association and told them to steer clear of you.'

'I thought Maureen at The Quill and Ink was a bit short with me this morning.' Ben took the offered cup of coffee, even though his stomach was still churning. 'So how come you were still prepared to meet with me today?'

'Because Rosie also told us what sort of offer you'd made her, and I'm ready to escape from this awful weather for good.' Black clouds were racing across the iron-grey sky outside the window, threatening to burst open at any moment. The thick frost that the Bay had woken up to had melted away, the temperature much milder, despite what felt like a brewing storm.

'I'm not sure I can make you quite as good an offer. This end of town isn't quite as prime a spot as where Belle's Bride's is located, but I'm sure Hemmingway's will be happy to come to some sort of arrangement.' The coffee was strong, and so hot that it burnt Ben's throat on the way down.

'As long as it's enough to persuade my sister Maria that it's the right thing to do, then we should be on.' Sebastian rubbed his hands together. Finally Ben had found someone in the Bay prepared to put money first. 'How soon do you think you can get the offer on the table?'

'Well I'm planning to head off tomorrow, so I'm hoping to get everything done by then. I'll ring the office when I get back to the hotel and call you to let you know as soon as I've had the offer from them.'

Ben stood up and shook Sebastian's hand. Maybe it was all because it had been so easy, or because the Tavernita had always been a second choice, but he didn't feel a tenth of the satisfaction he usually felt at closing a deal. It was definitely time to get out of the Bay.

* * *

Every time the bell on the shop doorway had sounded, Maddie's head shot up, half-expecting it to be Ben. She hadn't wanted it to be, of course; she'd already told him there was nothing he could say.

All the same, it had been a relief to shut the shop at the end of the day and to have somewhere to go. The last thing she wanted to do was just sit in the flat thinking about what an idiot she'd been, believing that her attraction to Ben had meant something significant.

The flat was a mess. She still hadn't stopped searching for that little wooden plane, as if finding the Christmas decoration that Becky had bought her might suddenly make everything right again. It could wait, though; getting to David's nativity play on time was far more important.

The sound of recorders playing 'Silent Night' carried across the primary school car park, as Maddie followed groups of parents and other relatives into the hall to take their seats. Becky was looking out for her, and waved her over as soon as she came through the door, a prime spot near the front of the audience already secured.

'You made it!' Kissing her on both cheeks, Becky gave her a hug. 'I didn't know if you would, after everything else that's been going on.'

'I wouldn't miss this for the world.' Maddie took the seat next to Becky and flicked through the programme that had been left on her chair. There was a cast list and pictures that the children had drawn, depicting the nativity, as well as the words to 'Good King Wenceslas', which the audience were expected to join in with at the end of the show.

The lively chatter of the audience drifted into silence as the curtains stuttered open. The little girl playing Mary — who was holding a hobby horse in lieu of a donkey — was led onto the stage by the boy playing Joseph.

Seconds later they were headed towards a Wendy house at the corner of the stage, as the narrator explained that the couple were looking for somewhere for Mary to have her baby, and that this was the tenth inn they'd tried. Joseph banged on the door of the Wendy house, and it was flung open with such enthusiasm that the little boy was almost knocked off his feet.

'Sorry, there's no room at the inn, but you can use the stable if you like.' David said the words with the biggest grin on his face that Maddie had ever seen; and, despite the misery of the last twenty-four hours, and the fear that Hemmingway's might still open up in the Bay, she smiled.

Turning to look at Becky, there were tears in her friend's eyes. This was what was really important, and it would take more than Ben Cartwright or Hemmingway's before she'd ever agree to leave the Bay. Whatever it took, she'd do all she could to stop them opening — organise a protest march, chain herself to railings — anything.

★　★　★

'He did such an incredible job.' Maddie handed Becky a paper plate when the interval started, a mince pie balancing in the middle. 'You must be so proud of him.'

'You wouldn't believe how much. I'm only sorry that Henry isn't here to see it. He was so worried after the meningitis that David would never be like other children, and he isn't — he's so much more than just ordinary.'

'He is, and so are you.' Maddie smiled, catching sight of one of David's teachers. 'And, given the way his teacher hasn't stopped looking at you all evening — Jack, isn't it — it seems I'm not the only one to think so.' Maybe romance wasn't completely dead after all.

'He asked me — well, us — to go to the Christmas Eve service with him. Do you think I should go?' Becky's cheeks were turning pink. 'I wanted to ask your advice, but I felt awful even mentioning it after everything with *he-who-shall-not-be-named*.'

'Don't be daft, and of course you should go.' Maddie broke a piece of pastry off her mince pie. It tasted like cardboard. 'He seems like a lovely guy, and David already thinks he's great.'

'I'm not about to rush into anything, but it does feel good to have something to look forward to again. Not that life with David and the shop isn't great, but I miss being part of a couple, having someone to share the ups and downs of the day with.' Becky almost dropped her mince pie as she turned towards Maddie. 'I'm sorry, I didn't mean . . . '

'It's alright. I know exactly what you're saying, and I agree. It just doesn't happen the way you expect, like it does in the books. Sometimes I think those stories have a lot to answer for.' She squeezed Becky's hand. 'You know that better than anyone.'

'True, although it's not just boy-friends who can throw a spanner in the works.' Becky raised an eyebrow. 'Maria was over here when you were queuing up for the refreshments, and she said she'd banned her brother from coming to see Manny in the nativity play. Apparently Sebastian's badgering her non-stop to sell the Tavernita and move back to Spain.'

'He's mentioned wanting to do that when I've been there before.' A cold sensation washed over her. 'I think he even said something about it when I was in the restaurant with Ben. You don't think they'd sell to Hemmingway's, do you?'

'Not whilst Maria has a breath in her body, I shouldn't think.' Becky was obviously keen to dismiss the idea. 'So I wouldn't worry about that.'

Maddie just nodded. Not worrying was easier said than done, though.

★   ★   ★

Thunder was rumbling when Maddie left the school, and she counted the gap between each flash of lightning and the sound that followed soon after — the gaps decreasing with every instance. Quickening her pace, she was only about two minutes away from the flat when the rain started to coming down with such force that it bounced off the pavements, almost immediately forming rivers of water that raced down the high street towards the sea. The waves crashing against the harbour wall could be heard from as far up as the top of the high street. She hadn't seen a storm like that in a long time. Maybe it was that thing they'd talked about at uni, when she'd been studying Thomas Hardy's novels — 'pathetic fallacy', where nature seemed to be reflecting human emotion — the stormy weather echoing her mood. Becky had tried her best to brush off Maria's comments about selling Martha's Tavernita, but it was a very real prospect, and that definitely warranted a storm.

Up in the flat, she took off the clothes that had been soaked through completely in the few minutes she'd been caught in rain. Having put on her pyjamas, she turned on the Christmas lights in the lounge as if she were on autopilot. Although it was only three days away, all the joy seemed to have gone out of Christmas this year. Even seeing David in the play had been tainted by further revelations about Hemmingway's and the likelihood that they hadn't finished searching for a venue in the Bay just yet. Would she even have a business in the New Year?

She couldn't sleep. When she'd tried to go to bed, even a warm drink and the drops of lavender oil she put on her pillow hadn't done anything to stop her mind racing. The thunder and lightning was still crashing outside, and the relentless thudding of the rain on the roof didn't exactly help.

She tried reading, but she wasn't taking any of the words in properly. She must have read the same page about ten times before giving up and walking back through to the lounge. Maybe watching television would help. There was bound to be an old black-and-white film on, or a repeat of some gameshow from the eighties, at this time of night — well, morning, if she was being strictly accurate.

Picking up the remote control, it dropped out of her hand as a huge crash made the windows rattle. The lightning must have struck something. Dashing back into her bedroom, she glanced out of the window that looked down towards the harbour. The retaining wall was still intact, but the waves were doing their best to leap over the top of it, and the boats moored there were being tossed about as though they weighed nothing at all.

There was no sign of anyone down near the harbour, but she was sure she could hear shouting over the rain still battering relentlessly against the roof above her.

Pulling on her coat and boots, she headed back down towards the front door, where water had begun to seep in and the mat was already wet through. Pulling the door open was like stepping on to a film set, it looked so surreal. She couldn't even make out where the pavement ended and the road started; it was as if the shop was on the edge of a rampaging river. And even more water was coming in, so she slammed the door shut again.

She needed something to try and stem the water, but it wasn't as if she kept sandbags in the flat just in case. Taking some pillows off the spare bed and some towels out of one of the cupboards, she tried to stop the water spreading any further. She was desperate to go into the shop and see what was happening in there, but there was nothing she'd be able to do, and the lightning was still illuminating the sky every few seconds.

Suddenly aware that her phone was ringing, she raced back up the stairs — there were already three missed calls.

'Maddie, you scared me half to death!' Rosie was almost shouting at the other end of the line. 'I've been calling you for the last ten minutes.'

'I didn't hear the phone, I've been trying to stop the water coming through the front door.' She looked down the stairs, pools of water already darkening the towels she'd laid on the floor.

'You're okay, though?'

'I'm fine. It's like another world out there. I don't think I've ever seen anything like it.' As she spoke, another crash of thunder sounded outside.

'I called Becky too, to check she and David were okay.' Rosie's voice was starting to return to a normal pitch at last. 'They're fine, but she said she'd had a call from a friend at the other end of the Bay, and apparently the bridge has gone.'

'What do you mean, it's gone?' Dickens Crossing straddled the river on the only road which led directly into the town. If something had happened to it, then the only way in and out by car would be through the Welham Valley, which was frequently prone to flooding, and more often than not the roads would be closed there after really heavy rain. The river was at its widest where it circled the Bay, and, although a few of the surrounding farms had small bridges that crossed the river further up, it was going to make it difficult to get in and out of a town that was little bigger than some villages. 'Her friend said it was hit by lightning and it just sort of collapsed: whole chunks of it were washed into the river.'

'I suppose I shouldn't worry about a bit of rain on the mat, then.' Maddie crossed her fingers that the shop wasn't suffering a worse fate. 'How are things are your place?'

'It seems fine so far, and Simon's been down into the shop.' Rosie sounded almost apologetic. Unlike Maddie's place, the shop at Belle's Brides was integrated with the flat, so you could go down to it through an internal door at the bottom of the stairs. 'Do you want me to send him over to take a look at your place?'

'Absolutely not. I'm not having Simon getting washed away on a river of rainwater on my conscience!' Maddie managed to laugh at the idea. 'As long as I know you're both safe and that Becky and David are okay, everything else can wait until the morning. I'll call you then, okay? Take care.'

Ending the call, Maddie shrieked as the lights went out. Another look through the bedroom window confirmed that they'd gone out all over town. Fumbling for her phone in the dark, it illuminated as she pressed the first button, and she managed to text Rosie to say she was okay, even in the dark. The last thing she wanted was to have poor old Simon knocking on her door to come and rescue her. She texted Becky, who replied to say they were fine and that David was curled up with her on the bed, and she wasn't intending to move anywhere until the morning. Following their lead, Maddie headed back into the bedroom and pulled the covers over her head, trying to drown out the sound of the rain, as she waited for it to get light.

10

Maddie must have drifted off eventually because, when she finally threw back the covers, the light in her bedroom was on and her alarm clock was flashing. The electricity had come on again during the night. Rain was still spattering against the window, but it was much gentler than it had been hours earlier.

Not stopping to get dressed, she pulled on the boots that she'd abandoned in the darkness of the lounge the night before and shrugged into the coat she'd been wearing, which was still wet and stuck to her pyjamas where it rested on her shoulders. Rushing down the steps, she braced herself for what the scene outside might look like, trying not to let her imagination extend to what state the shop might be in.

It wasn't as bad in the high street as

she'd thought it might be. The water was still rushing down the hill, but she could at least make out the edge of the pavement now, and the river of rain had slowed to a gentler pace.

Her fingers fumbled as she turned the keys in the three locks on the shop door, trying to resist the urge to press her face up against the glass to assess the damage. Pushing the door open at last, she sighed with relief. It was okay. There were a few floorboards that might need replacing, and she'd probably have to buy some industrial-strength cleaning fluid to get rid of the stale river-water smell that was already pervading the shop, but it could have been much worse. As luck would have it, the books occupied the space at the far end of the shop, and none of the water had travelled that far. Thinking about the beautiful dresses in Belle's next door, she only hoped Rosie had fared as well.

★　★　★

Ben had barely slept. He wanted to blame the storm, but there was more to it than that. He'd plugged his headphones into his iPod and turned it up to try and drown out the sound of the thunder and lightning — it was always a sound he'd always hated, ever since he'd been small — but the loud music hadn't exactly been conducive to sleep either. There'd been a bad feeling in the pit of his stomach ever since the row with Maddie, and every time he closed his eyes, her face swam into view — that look of pure contempt written across it.

Opening the curtains of his room when the light suddenly came back on, he couldn't believe what he was seeing. It was really early and still dark, but the security lights in the hotel grounds had come on too, illuminating a stretch of ground in front of them. He usually had a view down to the river and the old stone bridge that straddled it — which, before last night, had been at least a hundred feet long. Only now there was nothing there, and the river had spilled over its banks and onto the land either side. There was a large oak tree down too, its upper branches plunged beneath the surface of what Ben could only assume was the river — although it was almost impossible to make out where it properly began and which bits were just flood waters. Even with the iPod turned up to its maximum, it was amazing that he hadn't heard the bridge collapse.

Maddie was the first thought that came into his head as he took in how much damage the storm had really done. The building which housed Cecil's Adventures was old, and there was every chance it hadn't held up particularly well in such bad weather. Even if she didn't want to see him, he had to check she was still okay. He wanted to see if there was anything he could do — anything she'd let him do.

★　★　★

'What do you want? Come to gloat over the damage, I suppose.' Maddie had

201

just about had a chance to check out the shop and get dressed to start the clean-up, when Ben arrived on the doorstep of Cecil's Adventures. It was barely light outside, and most people were probably still tucked up in bed, recovering from the lost sleep of the night before. Yet here he was, bold as brass. If he made one comment about selling the lease or how much trouble it was sorting out a mess like the one the storm had left behind, she wouldn't be responsible for her actions.

'Do you really think that little of me?' He looked genuinely sad, but she'd stopped trusting anything he said days ago.

'What do you expect me to think?' She carried on mopping the floor. Looking into those brown eyes had been her downfall once before, and she wasn't about to repeat that mistake.

'Maybe it's best if we don't talk about that. Is there something I can do to help instead?' Ben was already lifting up one of the towels she'd put down when she'd first come into the shop, before she'd found the mop. He moved onto the pavement outside, wringing it out so tightly that it was only damp by the time he handed it back to her.

'Thanks.' She forced the word out, aware it sounded petulant. 'It's not too bad here, but I was going to check on Rosie's place, and then go down to Becky's shop. She's got some of her supplies in the cellar, so I've a horrible feeling it will be much worse down there.'

'I'm not sure either of them will be particularly pleased to see me in the circumstances.' He gave her a wry smile, and she had to fight quite hard not to return it.

'Neither was I, but you didn't let that stop you turning up here.'

'Fair point.' He laughed good-naturedly, and it was like the old Ben was back — the one who had volunteered to dress as an elf for the children — and had taken the place of the horrible version who was threatening to open a Hemmingway's and put her out of business.

Rosie was already in her shop when the two of them knocked on the glass.

'I was just going to come and see if you were okay.' She hugged Maddie, completely ignoring Ben, and whispered in her ear: 'What's he doing here?'

'We were just doing the same. It seems Ben here wants to become a knight in shining armour.'

'I can think of other names for him!' Rosie folded her arms across her chest. 'We're fine, anyway. There are a few leaks up in the flat, though, so we're just going to see if we can sort them out, and then find out if there's anyone else who needs a hand.'

'We're going to check on Becky and David, if you're okay. So I'll see you there later, probably?' Maddie gave her another hug. 'I'm just hoping the cellar hasn't totally flooded.'

Maddie could hear the distinctive sound of a water pump even before they got to Becky's shop. Ebenezer's Christmas Emporium was spread over two floors, with the flat in what had once been an attic, and the storeroom in the cellar. Becky opened the door, dark shadows under her eyes that suggested she'd had a sleepless night too.

'How's everything at your place?' It was definitely a water pump chugging away, but it was typical of Becky to ask how things were for Maddie first, even in the midst of a rescue operation in her own house.

'No real damage, so I was lucky. I take it by the sound of things that the cellar flooded?' She followed Becky in to the house, with Ben in her wake.

'Quite spectacularly. Luckily there was very little stock down there because we've been so busy and nearly all of the ornaments were already in the shop, but I think some of the wooden stairs have finally given up the ghost. So I'll have to get someone in for repairs as soon as possible.' Becky shrugged, as if worse things had happened. And for her they certainly had. 'Jack said he might be able to have a look for me, but to be honest, I don't think he's got any idea what he's doing, so I'd rather wait. Although heaven knows when I'll be able to get someone in, with everything shutting down for Christmas. Even the loss adjusters from the insurance firm can't come out until the twenty-ninth. Luckily, I kept the pump from the last time this happened. It was nearly ten years ago, but I can still remember the awful smell when everything started to dry out. That's why I wanted to be able to get up and down the stairs, to chuck out the old carpet and anything else that's water-damaged, before it starts to stink.'

'I could take a look.' It was the first time Ben had spoken since they'd gone into the building, and Becky spun round to look at him as if she hadn't noticed him before.

'You're not a builder.' Maddie was tempted to say something detrimental about what it was he actually did, but she pressed her lips together. Maybe he would be able to help Becky, and that was the important thing — at least for today.

'I'm qualified as a surveyor, and before that I did a lot of carpentry. I helped my dad make several sets of staircases as a kid. Even if I can only make it safe until the loss adjusters come out, that's got to be something — hasn't it?' He seemed to relax as Becky nodded. 'Just make sure you get some photos first — you don't want them trying to wriggle out of paying up.'

'I'll take you down to have a look, if you're sure?' Becky looked from Maddie to Ben and back again, as though she was waiting for her to give them permission.

'He might as well have a go, I suppose.' Maddie was torn between wanting Ben to fix Becky's problems, and seeing him fail miserably. She had a horrible feeling, though, that he was one of those people who'd turn out to be good at everything. 'I'll put the kettle on. Is David still asleep?'

'For now, but we better get a move on before he gets up, or he'll want to join in with the repairs.' Becky laughed. 'That boy watches far too much *Bob the Builder* for my liking!'

Maddie barely had time to fill the teapot before Becky was back in the kitchen. She looked exhausted, but still fussed around, making toast for them all and insisting that Maddie sit down.

'He's quite a dab hand with a hammer, you know. He's already taken the rotten treads off, and found spare wood down in the cellar from when I had some of the floorboards replaced in the upper floor of the shop. He thinks it should dry out fine.'

'Well, just don't start making him out to be some sort of hero. He's the enemy, remember.' Maddie stirred her tea a bit more vigorously than needed, sending some of it over the sides of the cup and into the saucer below.

'He isn't acting much like the enemy today.'

'If he worked for almost anyone but Hemmingway's, or even if he'd told me that from the start, I might be able to forgive him.'

'Forgive him?' Becky laughed. 'You wouldn't have let the poor bloke through the door. And he was only doing his job, remember; he's not an axe murderer or anything.'

'Working for Hemmingway's is worse in my book.' Maddie frowned. If she was acting like a child, then she couldn't help it. That was what children did when they thought something was unfair, wasn't it? Sulk. And the prospect of Hemmingway's opening in the Bay seemed about as unfair as it came.

'I'm just saying that maybe you should give him a chance.' There was that darn reasonable tone of Becky's again.

'A chance to what? He was never

interested in me, anyway. He only ever wanted to get his hands on the lease for Cecil's Adventures.' Maddie wasn't sure how much more stirring her tea could take. 'Anyway, he's due to go home today, so I don't suppose we'll see him again once he seals the deal on the Tavernita.'

'It's not going to be that easy to get out of town at the moment.'

'I'm sure he'll find a way. He's probably got a helicopter at his disposal, or he'll just knock one up from some old bits of wood he finds down in your cellar.' She had to laugh at the expression on her friend's face. 'Okay, I'll go and talk to him. See if he wants a cup of tea or something — but I'm not promising I won't stir it with the spoon you usually use to dish up the cat's food.'

* ★ ★

'You're obviously quite well-practised at this DIY stuff.' Maddie, who'd been determined to be unimpressed, couldn't quite manage it in the face of the brilliant job Ben had done at repairing the stairs. He'd been singing, too, as if he were actually enjoying himself rather than desperately trying to claw back some credibility.

'It must be like riding a bike. It's all coming back to me, almost as if my dad's still next to me whispering the instructions in my ear.' He looked up at her and she caught that same expression on his face which had been there once or twice before, like he really wanted to tell her something. 'I wanted to be just like him when I was growing up. He taught me everything I knew, and I was going to follow him into the family business.'

'What happened?' Maddie leant against the door frame at the top of the staircase, willing him to finish what he started. Somehow, it mattered to her to find out something about his past, even if he was about to walk out of her life for good — leaving only the legacy of an unwanted Hemmingway's behind.

'I told you he died, but what I didn't say was how sudden it was. He had a massive heart attack one day at work, and that was it. He died just before my thirteenth birthday.' Ben's voice betrayed his emotion, even after all this time. 'The business was up to the eyeballs in debt, and he had no life insurance. We lost everything, the house included, and Mum was convinced that it was carrying the secret of how badly the business was failing that killed him. It's been strange being here. Sarah-Jane's cottage reminded me of our old place so much, and then the parallels with Becky and David losing Henry . . . Only we didn't have the same sort of community to rally round, so it was up to me to grow up and take on some responsibility.'

'Oh, Ben, I'm so sorry. I had no idea that you'd had such a rough time' She really meant it, even if the words sounded hollow.

'It was a long time ago, but I suppose

it changed everything. Will was still a kid, and Mum had to go back to work — but she couldn't get a teaching job locally, so she took shift work, and we had to stay in a hostel for the first year. I had to take Will to and from school, and learn to run the house when we eventually got a flat of our own. It was hard on him too: he could never have the things he wanted for his birthday or Christmas, and he found out far too early that Santa doesn't always deliver what you ask for. I did my best and got a part-time job as soon as I could, and paid my own way through uni, too. I promised myself I'd get the best-paid job I could after that, to make life easier for Mum and Will, and that I'd never, ever let myself get into the sort of financial mess my father did, even if that meant I couldn't do the job I loved. I can't help feeling responsible for Will, even now, and renting Sarah-Jane's place for him made me feel like I was still doing my part.'

'I wish you'd told me all of this when

we first met.' It seemed like so much more than a couple of weeks earlier that he'd come into Maddie's life. 'So much more about you makes sense now.'

'It's not something I often share, but I just wanted you to know before . . . '

'Before you go, or before you finish the deal on the Tavernita for Hemmingway's?' The expression on his face changed as she spoke.

'You know about Sebastian wanting to sell?'

'His sister Maria is going to dig her heels in, you know, so you'll be in for a fight.' She was tempted to tell him about her plans to organise a protest march, but he answered before she could:

'I hope so.'

'Don't you want the lease?' If Maddie hadn't still be leaning against the door, her legs might have given way with the shock.

'Not any more. I'd get the sack if anyone overheard me say it, but I don't think a town like St Nicholas Bay is the right sort of place to open a Hemming-way's.'

'Can you convince them of that?' It was just as well he was still working on the rickety staircase, or she might have hugged him.

'I doubt it. What Hemmingway's want, they usually get, one way or another.'

'Hasn't anyone ever managed to stop them opening up? I was thinking, maybe we could organise a protest or something. I was planning to tie myself to the railings on the walkway at the side of the bridge — until it collapsed.' She laughed, even though she wasn't completely joking.

'There was one town, now I come to think of it . . . and actually, you've just given me an idea. I can't guarantee it will work, but I'll do my best to persuade them before I leave.'

'You're still planning on going today, then?'

'It depends if Maureen can let me stay on. I'm guessing any guests booked to check in tonight won't find it any easier to get into town than I will to get out.' He shrugged. 'But at least I can talk to the office before they close down for Christmas this afternoon, and if Becky could use the help, I'd like to come back later and help her get rid of the old carpet and anything else that needs chucking out.'

'Becky was right, you know.' Maddie's anger had all but melted away.

'About what?'

'You're not *all* bad.' She laughed again as his eyebrows knitted together, trying to work out if it was an insult or not.

★ ★ ★

Maddie's good mood appeared to have evaporated by the time Ben made it up to the kitchen. She was scrolling through her phone and muttering something in hushed tones to Becky, who in turn looked as white as a sheet.

'What's wrong?' He took the seat

next to Maddie, an expression of panic on her face as she turned to look at him. Something else must have happened in the storm.

'David only really wanted one thing for Christmas: the wooden castle that's been in the window of Tiny Tim's Toys since November.' She furrowed her brow when he didn't immediately react. 'Meg, who owns the shop, sold it to a family who collected it a couple of days ago. And she'd ordered another one for David that was going to be delivered today. Only the delivery company have just phoned her and said there's no way they can get it here. And they won't be making any more deliveries to the Bay until after the flood in the Welham Valley is completely clear.'

'It wouldn't be so bad if he hadn't asked Santa for it at the Gift Day. If I have to tell him that it won't arrive until after Christmas, I'll have to explain *everything* — the whole Santa thing — and that was a conversation I was hoping to put off for a good few years yet.' Becky had ripped the tissue she was holding into shreds as she spoke, and Maddie was still scrolling through her phone.

'There must be a supplier we can ring, someone who's prepared to make the effort to get into town?'

'It's no good, Mads, Meg's already spent half the morning calling everyone she can think of.'

'Was it the grey fort with all the soldiers, or a different castle?' Ben remembered seeing it because it had reminded him of the one his father had made for him years before. As Becky nodded, he thought about the pink castle resting in the boot of his car. With a coat or two of paint and some minor alterations, it might just about do the job. 'In that case, I think I might have a solution. I've got something similar for my niece in my car — it's the wrong colour, but that should be an easy fix. I won't be seeing her until after Christmas now, what with the flood, and I can replace it by then.'

'Really?' Becky leapt up and threw her arms around his neck.

'It's the least that one of Santa's elves can do in a situation like this.' He smiled as Becky finally let him go. 'Can you both come and meet at The Quill and Ink in about half an hour, and get some grey and black paint from somewhere, if you can?'

'Meg's bound to have some of that in the shop, or I can give Paul at Marley's Chains a ring, he'll definitely have some.' Meg was already scrolling through her phone again.

'I'll see you at the hotel, then?' Standing up to leave, he couldn't stop smiling. This Christmas spirit thing that seemed to cloak the Bay and its residents was in danger of getting addictive.

11

Ben was making his way up the hill, his mind whirring about how to adapt the castle. He was also trying to work out how to get out of the proposal Hemmingway's had put forward to buy the Tavernita following his call the afternoon before. Stopping as he drew level with the restaurant itself, he had to step back when the door opened and Maria shoved Sebastian out on the path to meet him.

'Tell him!' She gestured towards where Ben stood and Sebastian's face turn a deep shade of puce. 'If you don't tell him, I will!'

'Tell me what?'

'Our mother has had to step in and sort all this out, after he went behind my back to talk to you!' Maria was quivering with rage, and Ben had to suppress a smile. He'd never taken to

Sebastian — maybe it was the way he'd kept calling Maddie '*Bonita*' that night at the restaurant — but he felt a bit sorry for him, having to negotiate with his fiery sister.

'I'm sorry, but the deal's off.' Sebastian kept his eyes firmly focused on the ground as he spoke.

'So you'll have to find somewhere else for that lousy coffee shop of yours.' Maria turned towards him, her eyes almost black. 'My mother has given us both our inheritance now, so Sebastian can go to Spain, and I can carry on with the business and get it back up on its feet. It's not right, but it's done now, so the two of you can stop your little scheme.'

'Right, well, good luck.' He directed the comment at Maria, and had to fight the urge to kiss her in gratitude — a move which was unlikely to be received well in the circumstances. That was one obstacle out the way. Now he just had to persuade Hemmingway's that St Nicholas Bay wasn't a location worth pursuing, which might not be quite so easy without someone like Maria to fight the battle.

★ ★ ★

Maddie collected the paint from Tiny Tim's Toys and met Becky outside her shop, an hour after it had finally stopped raining. Jack had come down from his lodgings at the other end of town to help out with the clean-up in the cellar, and he was keeping David amused while the women set out on their secret mission to The Quill and Ink.

'Do you think this castle will be any good?' Maddie could picture the toy soldiers she had for David in the package under her tree. He'd talked non-stop about the castle on Gift Day and, if it had been possible to keep all her fingers and toes crossed that Ben could pull this off, then Maddie would have done.

'I hope so. I don't think Ben's the

sort to make promises he can't keep.' Becky smiled as Maddie rolled her eyes. 'Okay, I know he wasn't as honest with you as he could have been, but it wasn't like he actually promised you something else, was it?'

'No.' Maddie hadn't told Becky about the whole conversation she'd had with Ben in the cellar. After all, he'd said he didn't share the story about his past with many people, and it was his choice alone who to tell it to. But she had told her about Ben not wanting to open a Hemmingway's anymore, although that was something he hadn't made any promises about either.

The whole town seemed to have been galvanised into action following the storm, and there were people everywhere repairing the damage. The memorial tree had somehow survived intact, although the same couldn't be said for the stars that had hung there. Amazingly, the little wooden Christmas decoration that Becky had given Maddie was still there when she went down to check on it before picking up the paint, alongside the one that David had hung for this father. She'd been tempted to rescue the plane and take it home, but it belonged on the memorial tree.

To give the council their due, they'd already sent down a small team which was working on the bridge, presumably to prevent any more damage. It looked as though they were in the process of erecting a scaffolding walk way between the two sides of the river. Maybe Ben would be able to walk out of the Bay after all, picking up his car once the Welham Valley was clear. Funny how the thought of that wasn't nearly so appealing as it had been a few hours before.

The façade of The Quill and Ink didn't look like it had been badly harmed by the storm, and there was no sign of any water damage inside either. Maddie followed Becky into the foyer; Ben was already there, standing next to a fireplace, its mantel swathed in holly.

'Thanks for coming up. I would have brought it down, but I didn't want to risk David seeing it, and I'll need to leave it up here to paint it.' He tapped his nose. 'Actually, I'd better keep that under wraps; I don't want Maureen overhearing and kicking me out after all. She's agreed to let me stay on for now, since the guests who were booked into my room for the next three nights have cancelled.'

'You're not going home, then?' Maddie wondered if she sounded as relieved as she felt.

'I'll need to stay until at least tomorrow to give the paint a chance to dry — and, let's face it, St Nicholas Bay isn't the easiest of places to get out of at the moment.'

He held open the door that led to the stairwell, and they followed him up to his room on the second floor.

'Okay, before I lift the towel off, you've got to remember that I'll be repainting it, and it'll look totally different when it isn't candyfloss pink.'

Ben grinned. 'And I'll be cutting some arrow slits in the sides of the turrets.'

'Oh, Ben, it's fantastic.' Becky was the first to speak when he finally lifted the towel off. Maddie, for once was speechless. Even though it was exactly the shade of baby-pink he'd described, she could see how exquisitely made it was. The workmanship was incredible, even better than the one that had been on display in the toyshop window for so long.

'Where did you find it? It's beautiful.' As she finally found her voice, she trailed a finger up the side of the turret, which was as smooth as silk.

'Do you really think he'll like it? Won't he notice it's not the one he wanted?' Ben was already examining one of the pots of paint.

'Not when it's even better than the one he asked for. You'll have to let me know how much you paid for it — and your time, of course.' Becky was grinning, her relief tangible, and Maddie suspected no price would be too much to see David's face when he opened it on Christmas morning.

'I didn't pay for it, I made it — and I wouldn't dream of taking any money for it. I just want David to keep believing for as long as possible, and it's my duty as an elf to make sure that happens.' He winked at Maddie, and all of that easy charm she'd fallen for in the first place seemed to have come rushing back. Only this time she knew a lot more about him, what he'd been through, and she liked him all the more because of it. She still didn't know if his interest in her had been strictly business — and she wasn't about to ask — but, either way, she couldn't help how she felt.

'I can't believe you made this. You shouldn't be working for Hemmingway's with a talent like yours.' Unlike Maddie, Becky wasn't holding back, and for the second time in less than an hour she was throwing her arms around Ben. 'What can I do to say thank you?'

'There's really no need.'

'Well, at least promise me that if you're still in the Bay by Christmas Day, you'll join us for lunch? Maddie will be there.' Becky's grin widened even further. She was definitely trying to matchmake.

'Thanks, I'll bear it in mind . . . ' Ben paused. 'Although I'm not sure yet what will be happening by then.'

'The offer's there if you want it. In fact, after this, I'll cook you dinner any time you like.' Becky scooped up her bag, pulling out a business card and putting it on the table next to the castle. 'My number's on there. I'd better be going now, though, or Jack will think I've run off and left him with David for good. Are you going to open the shop today, Mads? I'm not sure whether to bother, as I should think everyone in the Bay who's going to put up a Christmas tree has done so by now. They'll have bought all the decorations they're going to buy, and it's not as if we'll be getting any tourists in town today.'

'I had a craft class booked in today with the mother and toddler group. They've got some half-finished Christmas cards in the shop, which I think are supposed to be for the dads, so I'll have to ring round and see whether they're still planning to come. I always thought it was scheduled a bit too close to Christmas anyway.' Maddie sighed, suddenly feeling exhausted. It had already been a long day. 'I could do without it, if I'm honest, and I could come and help out with the clean-up at yours then.'

'I think Jack and I can manage now that Ben's sorted the stairs, but you're welcome to come for a drink as soon as you're free.' Becky looped her bag over her shoulder. 'And you, of course, Ben.'

'Thanks, but I've got a date.' He smiled again, and Maddie's heart sank at his words. 'With several coats of paint and a hairdryer! But I'll text you as soon as I think it's ready to move.'

'See you later, then?' Maddie looked over her shoulder at Ben, who was already opening the first tin of paint.

'Uh-huh.' He didn't look up, and she was none the wiser about his feelings for her. Maybe that told her all she needed to know.

* * *

Ben finished the last of the first layer of grey paint and leant back to look at his handiwork. It had been strangely therapeutic, just layering on brushstroke after brushstroke. Like Maddie's granddad had told her about skimming the stones, the very act of getting caught up in something else had given him clarity. He could see the best tack to take with Hemmingway's now. And, after a quick phone call to the Bucket and Spade pub, which sat right on the beach in Briony Bay, only a few miles along the coast, he had a more than viable alternative, too.

Whilst the first coat of paint was drying, he opened his laptop. It took him over an hour to get all the figures looking as convincing as they'd need to. The last thing he did was to upload a photograph he'd taken on his phone of the collapsed bridge. It was his trump card — if this didn't work, nothing would. Even if he refused to scout for any more properties in the Bay, someone else would be sent in his place. The only chance they had was if he could persuade them that Briony Bay would be a more profitable location, and he just hoped that the acquisitions director would pick up the message before he left for his Christmas holiday. He didn't stand a chance with Maddie until he'd put this right, and having that chance was the only thing he really wanted for Christmas.

12

Much to her disappointment, Maddie's craft class had decided to come into the shop after all. The mums had been determined; it was a way of keeping the children entertained whilst the ground was still too wet for them to go outside, even though the surface water had all but disappeared. By the time she'd made it over to Becky's to try and help out, they'd already got the cellar straight too — thanks in no small part to the repairs that Ben had done on the staircase. Jack couldn't do enough for Becky either, and Maddie had a feeling that it wouldn't be long before the trainee teacher was a permanent fixture in her friend's life.

She hadn't heard from Ben but, after a large glass of wine round at Becky's, she'd texted him instead to ask how the castle was going. He'd replied with a photo — which looked so amazing that Becky had poured them another glass to celebrate — but he hadn't said much else.

She didn't bother opening the shop on Christmas Eve. Usually it would be thronging with tourists up until closing time, but with the bridge destroyed and the road through Welham Valley still closed, there just wasn't the demand. Most of the locals knew they could knock at the flat if they needed a last-minute present, so it didn't seem worth opening up.

She called her parents in Cornwall to wish them a happy Christmas. They had half her father's family descending on them for the big day — he was one of six brothers — so she wanted to catch them before it got really hectic.

After the call, she wrapped the last of her Christmas gifts and put the finishing touches to the chocolate log and Christmas cake she'd promised to take around to Becky's the next day. She'd added another length to the log when Rosie and Simon had announced they'd be coming too. They'd been due to go to Rosie's parents — who really knew how to put on a spread — but, given the difficulty of getting out of the Bay, everyone's plans seemed to be changing. There was always the chance that Ben would be joining them too, but she was trying not to think about that too much.

* * *

Ben pressed his fingers against the side of the now-grey castle to check that the last layer of paint was definitely dry. The residents in the room next door must have thought he'd spent half the night styling his hair: he'd had the hairdryer running for hours, and at one point it had cut out altogether until it cooled down. Confident that the castle was now safe to move, he picked up his phone to text Becky and let her know.

Checking his emails, he saw there was one from Hemmingway's. Holding his breath, he clicked on the icon to open it. He had to read it three times to make sure he'd got it right, but it was there in black and white. Opening his laptop, he dashed off a reply in less than five minutes — his resignation. Between the painting and the few hours of sleep he'd managed to grab, he'd made up his mind — if he got the verdict he was expecting from Hemmingway's, he'd resign. In the end, it had been easy, and all the angst of the night before drained away as soon as he hit the Send button. Whatever else happened, it was the right decision.

After Becky and Jack had picked up the castle — and she'd cried, and begged him to reconsider her offer for dinner — the only person he wanted to see was Maddie. Even if he'd blown it for good, he had to tell her one more thing before he left.

Becky had told him that Maddie was taking David down to the crib service in the chapel, so that he didn't see the castle when they took it home, and that they were meeting her down there. Anticipating how cold it would be at the harbour, even inside the chapel, he looked in the hotel wardrobe for his scarf, but it wasn't there. He remembered having it on the Gift Day, just before he'd changed into his elf costume, and the holdall he'd taken down there with his change of clothes was still sitting at the bottom of the wardrobe. Reaching inside for his scarf, his hand made contact with something hard inside one of the zipped pockets. Lifting it out, he smiled — it was the perfect excuse to talk to Maddie. He just had to make one more stop on the way.

★ ★ ★

The scent of clove and orange from the recent Christingle service still filled the air as Maddie stood near the front of the chapel with David's hand in hers. He was watching, fascinated, as some of the congregation took on the roles of

Mary, Joseph and the innkeeper.

'He's not saying it right, Auntie Mads.' David spoke in a loud stage whisper, as the man who was supposed to be the innkeeper mumbled something about his hotel being full. 'He's supposed to say there's no room at the inn!'

'Sshh, David, he'll hear you.' Becky who was on his other side gently rebuked her son, but she was laughing, and so were the people in the row behind. David was far more entertaining than anything that was going on at the front of the chapel, and you couldn't be miserable for long when he was around. Quite often the crib service had to be held on the harbour-side, because the chapel was so small, but with far fewer visitors around than usual, as least they were able to stand in the relative warmth.

Maddie still hadn't heard from Ben, but Becky had told her just how stunning the castle looked, and she couldn't wait to see David's face in the morning, imagining him spending hours lining up his soldiers against the castle battlements.

The door of the chapel opened with a noisy creak just as the vicar was talking about the importance of showing hospitality at Christmas — even to strangers — and likening it to the need to pull together after the recent storm. Turning to see who it was who'd arrived just minutes before the service was due to end, she saw Ben slip into a row right at the back of the chapel.

Willing the vicar to hurry up with his notices — it was Christmas Eve, after all, and she couldn't have been the only one desperate for the service to end — Maddie forced herself not to turn around again to check Ben was still there.

Finally emerging on to the harbourside, she couldn't see him at first, but he was standing by the memorial tree that still was illuminated with a thousand lights, despite the storm taking its toll on the handwritten stars.

Becky, Jack and David seemed to instantly melt away, and suddenly she was standing opposite Ben, away from the rest of the crowd.

'I think I've got something of yours.' He lifted a small wooden ornament out of his pocket — the plane that Becky had bought her. Her eyes darted to the memorial tree behind him, wondering if he'd taken the other one down, but it was still hanging there.

'Where did you find it? I thought I'd lost it on Gift Day!' He put it in her hand as she spoke, and she curled her fingers round it.

'It was in the outside pocket of my holdall. I'm guessing you put it there by mistake, when it was next to the bag with your books in?'

'I must have done.' She looked at the little wooden man sitting in the cockpit of the plane, and he was smiling — she hadn't noticed that before. If she'd been looking for a sign when she wrote that message in the sand, maybe this was it.

'I wanted to thank you, not just for this, but for everything with David, before you left, and for saying what you did about Hemmingway's setting up in the Bay, even if it doesn't change anything.' She took his hand in hers, and his warm brown eyes crinkled in the corners, in the exact same way that had got to her the first time he'd walked into Cecil's Adventures.

'Actually, it did change something. I found an alternative venue in Briony Bay, and the report made the figures look so good it was a no-brainer for them. They've got a policy not to open another branch within less than ten miles, so it had to be Briony or St Nicholas. I think the picture of the bridge on the main road lying in a pile of rubble had to be the clincher, though. I told them there just wasn't the infrastructure to support the level of business they want, which was the same argument that persuaded them to pull out of that other town. We've got a lot to be thankful to that storm for.' He was grinning, and she should have felt ecstatic too, but the thought of him leaving weighed heavily all the same.

'The storm definitely changed some things, but I guess you'll be going as soon as the valley road reopens?' As she spoke, he tightened his grip on her hand and she looked up at him, willing him to say what she wanted to hear.

'There's no rush for me to go anywhere. I resigned from Hemmingway's when I got the confirmation they were going to take the site in Briony Bay.' He pulled her closer to him. 'I realised when I was painting that castle for David that I'd never be really happy if I didn't at least try to make a go of things doing something I loved. I've had enough ridiculous bonuses over the years to give me a really good cushion to start something up. As soon as I was sure I didn't need to work on them to get them to change their mind about the Bay, I was free to go.'

'What are you going to do?' Holding her breath, she waited for an answer.

'I'm buying the lease to Rosie's shop. I'm going to sell hand-made furniture and bespoke items — maybe even the odd fort. Although I'm not about to try and put Tiny Tim's Toys or any other local shops out of business. I've been down that route before.'

'Anything else?' She forced herself to keep looking into his eyes, trying to read what was written there.

'There's this girl who lives locally who I'd really like to take out.' Placing his hand on the small of her back, he pulled her another step closer. 'So, what do you think? Shall we finally have that meal at Nachos on the Bay once it's open again after Christmas?'

'It's a date.' Closing the final inches of space between them, she whispered in his ear: 'But, in the meantime, I'll settle for a kiss.'